SEAN GRISWOLD'S HEAD

SEAN GRISWOLD'S HEAD

Lindsey Leavitt

SCHOLASTIC INC.
New York Toronto London Auckland
Sydney Mexico City New Delhi Hong Kong

ISBN 978-0-545-40104-3

12 11 10 9 8 7 6 5 4 3 2 1   11 12 13 14 15 16/0

Printed in the U.S.A.   40

First Scholastic printing, October 2011

Book design by Danielle Delaney

To Curry,
Every day I love you.
But today, you get a book.

SEAN GRISWOLD'S HEAD

ONE

Nothing creates a buzz like an Executive Deluxe day planner. Not that I have much experience with buzzes, especially of the chemical variety, but my brother did double-dose me on NyQuil once when I was eleven. That thirty or so minutes of faint inebriation had nothing on this feeling. Pure, organized bliss.

I hug the planner to my chest and slowly brush the leather. It'll cost me a third of my Christmas money, but this baby has monthly *and* weekly calendars, financial graphs, to-do checklists . . . and did I mention the sweet, sweet leather?

"I can't believe you are spending that much money on an organizer, Payton." My best friend, Jac, leans against the store counter. We're at the mall, taking advantage of post-Christmas sales, and I'm itching to prep my organizer for the new year. "You can get an electronic one for like fifty bucks more. And what do you really need to plan, anyway? You're a freshman, not a CEO."

I smile serenely at my cute, ignorant friend. "I can't use my new highlighting system on a computer screen. And there's something about crossing off a task with a nice ballpoint, you know?"

"No. I really don't. But I love you all the same."

Of course she doesn't get it. Jac just spent eighty dollars on these ridiculously impractical red boots that will match two outfits, tops. Now, my well thought-out purchase? I'll use it *every day*.

"So you probably aren't interested in my highlighting system for our English readings. It's genius, really. Yellow for literary devices, pink for plot points, orange for conflict—"

"Why orange?"

"Because I look like crap in that color. I'd fight anyone who made me wear it."

Jac nods. Clothing—now that's something she understands. "Why not save the school stuff until we're actually back *in school*."

"Midterms are only a few weeks away."

"So let's enjoy our freedom while we have it." Jac fingers a green wallet. "I'm actually surprised your parents didn't get you a planner for Christmas. They're usually, like, the best present-givers. Unlike my parents. This is the third Christmas in a row that my dad gave me diamond earrings."

"Diamonds. Whoa. Daddy McThrifty strikes again."

"Hey, I was going to regift them to you for your birthday, but—"

"Okay. Yes. That does suck. In a non-sucking way."

"You know what I mean." Jac checks the price tag on the wallet and sticks it back on the shelf. "Your parents know you as, like, an actual person. It's almost weird how functional you all are."

"True. But my dad got me a book on rocks. I haven't collected rocks since I was ten. TEN. If he had it his way, I would still be four. I bet he slipped antigrowth hormones into my eggnog last week."

Jac giggles. "You hate eggnog." Her phone buzzes with a text. She checks it and points toward the counter. "We better hurry, schnookums. My sister's waiting and I want to walk by Cinnabon again and see if Hot Freckle Boy checks me out."

I hand the cashier my money with a post-holiday coupon and tuck my new planner into my messenger bag. Once we're by the food court, Jac achieves her desired catcall. And yes, I'm positive it's directed at her. I might get an occasional look from guys, but Jac . . . Jac gets the whistles.

Fifteen minutes later, she leans out the window of her sister's Jeep. "Call me tonight! I need you to tell me what happens in *A Tale of Two Cities* before break ends."

"You could read it, you know. Or buy the CliffsNotes."

"Forget Cliff. Payton Notes are much better."

I laugh. "I bet you wouldn't say that if Cliff was cute."

"He'd have to be way cute to pull off a name like Cliff."

I hug her good-bye and race into the house, excited to show off my toy to Mom and Dad. They're always teasing me about my organizational skills, but I know they love my neurotic tendencies. They never have to worry if I'll get my homework done.

"Dad!" I call. "I've taken anal retentive to a whole new level! Mom?" I bounce through the hallway, photos of the family from now back to my great-grandfather's infancy watching me as I go. No one. I peek into the garage. My brother Trent borrowed

Mom's minivan because he claims it delivers the ladies. Dad's Acura waits alone in the darkness.

Huh. They were home when I left. Maybe they went on one of their ever-increasing walks along the Schuylkill River. They've been kind of weird lately, out together day and night. Gazing at each other like they do in a bad soap opera during a long good-bye.

Sometimes, I get a little worried that something is seriously up.

I mean, they're always pretty lovesick around each other, but what if it's more? A good soap opera would throw in a murder cover-up or an unplanned love child. Which would be gross, because that means my parents are still capable of . . . doing the act that produces babies.

I hear murmuring coming from the bathroom, then laughter. My paranoia melts. They're laughing. Just like always. In fact, Mom's probably shaving Dad's head, a biweekly event almost as entertaining as color coordination. I jiggle the doorknob, and since it's unlocked, throw the door open. "Hey, baldy!" I sing. Then stare.

My dad is bent over the toilet seat, pants pulled down just enough that I see the top of his left butt cheek. Mom is standing behind him with a hypodermic needle in her right hand, poised to make a poke. They both startle when I barge in. Mom jerks so the needle grazes Dad's skin. His pants slide lower and I almost see Way Too Much. I slam the door shut.

Not paranoid. Something was up. But I thought "something" was more along the lines of my parents sharing a cute midlife crisis. Not shooting each other up with *drugs*.

4

"Payton!" Mom yanks the door back open. "Honey! Wait!"

I'm still standing at the door, my mouth hanging lower than my father's pants. He's behind her in a second, fumbling with his zipper. "Sunshine. Let's go to the living room. We need to talk."

♥ ♥ ♥

There is talking, but none by me.

The good news: My parents aren't drug addicts.

The awful, horrible, what-the-freak-just-happened-to-my-life news: The needle was filled with medicine. Medicine for my father's multiple sclerosis, aka MS. A disease that, up until about ten minutes ago, I was completely unaware he had.

"We're sorry we didn't tell you—" Mom starts.

"And we were going to!" Dad says, flopping down next to me on the leather couch. Mom stands behind him, arms folded. "We were just—"

"—waiting for the right time. There's still so little we know about it. We wanted to get a clearer idea of where this was going. And now to find out like this—"

"—we wish you hadn't—" Dad says.

"—but since you did—"

"—we'll just have to make the best—"

"—of an unfortunate situation," Mom finishes.

Unfortunate situation? Are they *kidding* me? It's a crippling disease. Isn't it? I've always lumped it in there with cerebral palsy and Parkinson's and . . . a bunch of other diseases I really don't know anything about.

5

Seriously. Unfortunate situation. Highlight that line yellow for use of a literary device: Crude Understatement.

"Well, I'll just spill it." Dad sighs when I give no sign of responding, other than finally closing my mouth to relieve my aching jaw. "The numbness in my left hand started last spring when your mom and I went to Cancun. It went away when we came home so . . . I didn't do anything." Dad picks at a loose string on his T-shirt. "I forgot about it. Tried to forget about it. But then, during the summer, my hand started tingling again. For weeks. And I kept it to myself, just like I've kept the fact that I've felt . . . off . . . tired for years.

"I finally told your mom and got tested and they found these sheath lesions—they're kind of like tumors—on my spine. The doctor sat us down and told us about MS."

Tingling. Numbness. Tumors.

Mom eases down next to me and smoothes my hair. I flinch.

"I know it all sounds scary, but there're different kinds of MS. Right now, your father will have a relapse, then go into remission, then relapse again. So far they've been spread out— it's still a manageable case. But some people"—Mom glances at Dad—"decline faster. Continually. It can get better, or it could get worse. Nothing is predictable. So this medicine helps. Well, he just started, so we hope . . . we hope it'll help."

Summertime. Like six months ago. That's how long they've known. They *knew*. And I had no clue. No clue. How . . . how *could* they?

"*Mi sol*, there is no way to tell you how sorry we are," she adds. "We feel horrible. I guess there never really is a right

6

time to hear this. We told your brothers, and then we were going to tell you too. We just hadn't decided . . . when."

They told my *brothers*? There's a steady pounding in my ears, and my stomach—no, my guts—feel like I've swallowed a kitten and the little fur ball is trying to claw his way out. This is such crap. Parents don't keep things like this . . . how could they have . . . and my brothers knew! This somehow makes it even worse. Once again, I feel like I'm just this stupid little girl. They all shared in this knowledge, walking around *knowing* while I just continued on with my regular life. Everything they've said is tainted now. Every day was a lie.

I'm going to explode in a minute. Explode from the pain.

Dad paces. "I know how much you worry about things. Remember the time I sprained my ankle in pickup basketball and you called every orthopedic surgeon in the city? I didn't want you worrying about me until we had a more concrete plan." Dad stops pacing and kneels down in front of me. "Sunshine, I can't even begin to tell you how sorry I am. I'll fill you in from here on out. Every detail. Things are going to be fine. I promise. All right?"

My mom shifts on the couch. "Is there anything you want to say?"

I leave without answering and lock myself in the bathroom. Dad's medicine is still balanced on the sink. I knock it over. *I promise.* Yellow highlighter again—irony. How could they promise me the truth when my whole family has lied to me for the last six months? Six months I spent believing everything was as perfectly aligned as my highlighting system, not blackened with an unknown illness.

7

I lean over the toilet bowl and throw up.

Fine.

Fine was my color-coded life before. Things will never be *fine* again.

TWO

I'm sitting in a vinyl chair outside the school guidance counselor's office, tapping my foot in rhythm to the smooth hits station blaring from the secretary's computer. The note that got me out of Spanish didn't say why I'm meeting the counselor for the first time, but I already know what this is about. It's been two weeks since I've said one word to my parents. Two weeks since I found out about my dad. So my mom, no doubt, called the school, asked what resources they had for parents who screwed up and need another adult to come in and fix it, and arranged this little meeting. A meeting I wasn't going to let happen.

Ms. Callahan rushes into her office, coffee mug in hand. "Payton! I'm so glad you're here! Won't you follow me?"

I stop tapping my foot and plant it firmly on the Berber carpet. "No. I won't."

Ms. Callahan, who is already halfway through her door, does a double take. "You won't?"

"I'd rather not. Uh . . . Fifth Amendment." I have no clue if the Fifth Amendment can really save me from unwanted guidance, but she sits down next to me, so it must apply. God bless you, Founding Fathers.

"Well, I suppose we can schedule another meeting later. But there *will* be a later. I've spoken with your mother about your father—"

I glance up at the secretary to see if she's listening. She's typing and grooving away to Lionel Richie.

"—and so I want us to set up some friendly chats. Since today wasn't planned, I'll give you this and we can meet up to talk about it tomorrow."

She digs through a monogrammed canvas tote and finally comes up with an orange-striped notebook. I snort. Orange is my highlighter color for conflict. Of course.

"It'll help you open up a little. Until you're ready to talk. It's a Focus Journal."

I stare at her blankly. Focus. I don't need this. I can *focus*. I'm the Queen of Focus. Well, former queen. Princess maybe. Duchess. Oh, who am I kidding? These last two weeks I've been so lost, I couldn't cook in the Royal Focus Kitchen.

"What am I supposed to do with it?"

"You write your Focus Exercises in it. So you pick something to focus on. It can be anything. A memory, a place, even something as basic as a pencil sharpener. You don't have to tell me what it is—we'll just call it your Focus Object. Once you've detailed your reactions and emotions on something you're not emotionally invested in, you should be ready to start addressing deeper issues."

I run my fingers along the spiral binding. Right. Like

10

describing the door in my Spanish class has anything to do with the fact that my dad's hand gets so messed up he can't even turn a doorknob.

♥ ♥ ♥

The next day, Miss Marietta wheels a TV across our biology classroom and I plunk my head down on my desk. I didn't mind TV time in elementary school. I looked forward to it. Really, I could watch a Stop, Drop, and Roll rap video a million times over. But a documentary on cell division in freshman biology? Not so much.

But it does give me an entire period to work on my Focus Exercises, which I'm supposed to present to Ms. Callahan next period. I've decided to meet with her, partially because I'm curious, and partially because I'm scared that if I don't, she'll write something horrible on my flawless permanent record, which would keep me from getting into a good college, which would limit my job options to trimming mustaches at Supercuts and my dating options to the creepy guy who sweeps up the hair. Even the Fifth Amendment couldn't save me then.

I turn to the first sheet of paper in my new notebook and count down ten lines—there are twenty-nine on standard notebook paper, so ten lines is a third of the way down. You know, give or take.

PAYTON'S FOCUS JOURNAL

On the next page I write . . .

I pause. Topic. Suck. This woman gives me a notebook; why couldn't she have given me a topic? Really, how is one object going to fix my family and life and mental condition anyway?

The voice of the video narrator drones on about the miracle of cell division. I doodle an amoeba in the corner of the page. Miss Marietta has her head down on her desk. Ah, maybe I could write about her.

Topic: Miss Marietta

Miss Marietta is new and trying to save the world one organism at a time. But once a month, she puts on some random video and takes a nap in the corner. We call these days "Hangover Thursdays" because the first Wednesday of every month is Ladies' Night at the local clubs. It is here that Miss Marietta trades in her world of microscopes and lab reports for a night of dancing and drinking. I know this because Jac's sister sees her out all the time, and apparently Miss Marietta is a closeted wild child. I told my parents about it back when we were speaking, and

*they were beyond scandalized. Who cares
what she does in her personal life, so long as
she keeps sticking in the videos?*

Nope. Won't work. That's all I know about Miss Marietta, all I *want* to know, right there.

I tap my pencil. Topic. I could write about all the MS clues I didn't pick up on over the last six and a half months. Dad's lunch breaks that turned into nap time. The doctor visits I thought were dental conferences. How Dad was always sick on Sundays because of the medication's side effects. How he asked me to help him with the can opener, probably because his hand was numb. How my parents were gone all the time. How I knew something was up but had no clue it was *this*. How I charged him one time when we were practicing for my school basketball tryouts and he stayed down longer than normal and that probably made his MS worse.

No. I've already chosen not to go THERE. I went there when I walked into that bathroom, and now the incident is safely filed in the Do Not Process cabinet of my brain. The file's contents might mention how stupid I feel that I didn't know, how mad I am at my parents . . . at everyone, not to mention scared and lonely and just . . . yeah. Focus Journal or not, I'm not going THERE again. Drawer locked.

The only way I can really approach this is to pretend it's a school assignment. So, we just talked about the writing process in English. Before you write, you prewrite. Brainstorm.

I rip out a sheet of notebook paper and draw a word web.

Now I just need inspiration. I survey the classroom, noticing first the pink suede jacket Sarah Sheckler is sporting that literally puts the as(s) in *nasty*. I sigh and write *school uniforms* in the web, drawing a separate line to add my belief that uniforms would create social balance in this district and save poor Sarah from herself. Except I already expressed this revolutionary idea in my student council speech, and I lost. So writing about it again might make me bitter. Well, more bitter than I am now.

I consider actual objects, writing them down as I see them. The dry-erase board, the TV, a model of an atom, the lab jars in the back filled with who knows what. Oh! I could go abstract and write about the hallways and make it some metaphor for the path of life. But then Ms. Callahan might read too much into it and think I'm suicidal on top of being in denial. Or whatever clinical term I've been labeled with.

What I need is something that has concrete details like an inanimate object but changes somehow. Like a living, breathing person.

Brynn McCabe, who sits across from me, chomps on a piece of gum. I add Brynn and gum to my list. Brynn's like Violet on *Charlie and the Chocolate Factory*, always chewing or talking or talk-chewing. And she spits while she does it. I'd have to wear rainwear all the time if she were my Focus Object. No dice.

Jac catches my eye and holds something up. It's a nearly dead-on mask of Miss Marietta's face. I giggle. She probably spent the whole video designing it, and somehow she knew it was just what I needed after my Ms. Callahan chat. I spell JAC out in bubble letters and fill it in with flowers. If I were to graph our friendship out, Jac and I might not make sense. We have different interests, fit into different cliques, but the length of our friendship makes most of that unimportant. You go through enough with a person over a long enough period of time and they just become a part of who you are. I guess I could write about all that but . . . someone like Jac deserves a novel. A series.

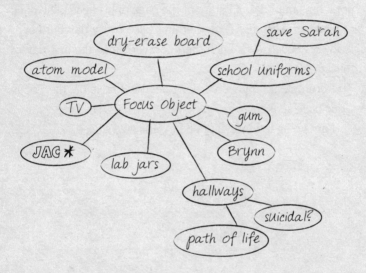

The video ends and Miss Marietta flicks on the lights, releasing a small moan from the class as everyone wakes up from their video-induced hibernation.

Class is over. Great. I have no Focus Object and thus no complete assignment. Before the Big MS Lie, I never neglected to turn in an assignment. Even the extra-credit ones. Even the ones I made up based on the teacher's lack of lesson depth.

Sean Griswold, the guy who sits in front of me, turns around and smiles. "I can never focus on the videos, can you?"

My whole body goes rigid. "No . . . no. No, I can't."

He nods and turns back around.

He said focus. The word *focus*. I hear angels singing. Everything goes dark except for a light that beams down on Sean. It is a God-given sign—like when people see the Virgin Mary in their grilled cheese, except this isn't religious and I'm actually not a big fan of dairy. I stare at the back of his head. The back of his head. His HEAD. Something I see every day but never really *see* because it's been there forever. Since the first day of third grade.

I crumple up my web. I don't need it. Praise be, the Focus Gods have spoken.

I am going to write about Sean Griswold's head.

THREE

Payton's Focus Exercise
January 17
Topic: Sean Griswold's Head Outline

I. Introduction
    A. Because of our alphabetical connection
       (Gritas/Griswold—just try to squeeze
       a last name between us), I've stared
       at the back, the profile, and occasionally
       the front of Sean's head since third
       grade.
    B. It's a perfect thing to focus on, because
        1. The environment is constantly shifting.
        2. I see it a lot.
        3. The Focus Gods told me to. You
           don't mess with the Focus Gods.

II. Body (er, rather, his Head)
   A. Hair
      1. Very blond, like a little kid's. Light bounces right off of it. White, almost.
      2. Soft. Like fuzz on a duckling. Not that I've touched it! But I might need to, once I get further into my research.
   B. Size
      1. HUGE.
      2. Is that mean? It's bigger than most heads, slightly off proportion from the rest of his body. He's gotta have a strong neck.
      3. Big enough that I have to crane my neck to see around his dome.
   C. Things it could fit into
      1. Toilet—yes.
      2. Batting helmet—heck no.

III. Conclusion
   A. I still don't see how writing about a head will
      1. Fix my family drama.
      2. Reorganize my life.
      3. Accomplish anything.
         a. Except writing in outline form

again is soothing, like walking
through the Tupperware aisle
in Target.
   b. Ahhhhh.
B. Seven years of staring and it's still the
   same old head, just like it's the same old
   haircut, and just like—as far as I know—
   it's the same old Sean Griswold.

♥ ♥ ♥

Ms. Callahan's office is anarchy, with books, paper, and dust stacked in random piles. The wall behind her echoes the chaos—pictures of students, inspirational quotes, and Post-its all surround a poster of the solar system with "Greystone High Counselor of the Universe" scrawled across it. There's a sickly sweet odor, something akin to a rotting orange smothered in ketchup. If I ever get over my own mental clutter, I'm going to devise a filing system for her beyond chair, desk, and ground. I might have to begin by explaining what exactly a file *is*.

She clears one of the piles off a chair and motions for me to sit. "Did you find a Focus Object?"

"I think so."

She smiles. Poor woman. Eyebrows gone wild, muddy lipstick, and legs ashier than Pompeii. If physical appearances send a message about our character, hers would be—*I have a hairy cat and buy my makeup at the dollar store.*

"Great. Since these are personal and I won't be reading them,

I want you to ask yourself this—is it something you can really dissect?" She taps her fingers on her desk. "Something you can really explore?"

"Yeah, I'm all set."

"You'll be amazed how this promotes growth. Why, one of my former students chose cows as his Focus Object and now he's on the national 4-H board."

So I write about a head and someday I'll be a neurosurgeon? Not quite. "Are we done?"

"Sure. I just wanted to check in with you. Here's a pass." She pushes the paper across her desk. "How are things going at home?"

I pick up the pass, taking a colony of dust bunnies with it. I have an intense desire to wash my hands. To wash my whole body. "Same old."

"And your dad?"

I glance at the clock. "They haven't discovered a cure for MS yet. I better go. I have to stop at my locker before next period."

Ms. Callahan leans across her chair and stretches out her arm like she's going to touch me. I shrink away.

"All right, Payton. I look forward to our next meeting."

That makes one of us.

FOUR

The next morning, I literally lose myself in my closet looking for a sock. Which leads me to the question—where do lost socks *go*? I bet if you corralled all the renegade socks and stitched them into a blanket, it'd cover more of the earth than the waning ozone layer. Not that I'm worried about the world's sock crisis. I hardly have time to find one matching pair. I have to get to school and begin my more in-depth analysis of Sean's dome.

"I can't afford another tardy. Come on," Jac says, dodging a flying hanger.

I poke my head out from my disaster of a closet. "Walk by yourself if you can't wait."

"Walk by myself? And risk catching social leprosy?" She sighs. "I'll wait."

"Sorry. Almost done." I push some old books into another corner. "Hey, since when did you become the President of Punctuality?"

"Since you can't even match your socks, let alone an outfit.

I mean, I've never even seen your bed unmade, and now this room looks like it's exploded. And I love you, but, seriously—what's with the sweater?"

I look down at my ensemble and shrug. Sure, green argyle and red cords might not be fashion forward, but at least it's clean. Kind of clean. It has a weird locker room stank and an orange crust on the collar. Maybe it was supposed to be in the dirty pile, not the clean pile heaped next to it. "They're just clothes."

Jac recoils like she's been slapped. "*Just* clothes?"

There's a tap on my bedroom door and my mom peeks her head in. "You girls are going to be late for school if you don't leave in the next five minutes."

I bury my head under some laundry. It's too early to face her Colombian temper.

"And I'm going to call Ms. Callahan and make sure you attend all your appointments," Mom says more loudly. "She said she had three meetings yesterday and she still managed to fit you in."

"Found it!" I ignore my mom and wave a purple striped sock in the air. Jac scrunches up her nose and shakes her head.

Mom sighs. "Payton, I know Ms. Callahan has a reputation for being . . . unorthodox, but if you aren't going to talk to us, you need to at least give this an honest try."

Honest. Huh. I might not read many parenting magazines, but I'm guessing there aren't too many articles entitled "How to Send Your Kids to a Deranged High School Guidance Counselor After They Find Out You Lied to Them! Ten Easy Steps." So I'd like to know where my mom got the revolutionary idea that talking to Ms. Callahan during my much-needed nutrition

22

breaks is going to get me to talk to them. What would I even say? Dad, your butt isn't as hairy as I would have thought. Mom, you're so good with a needle you should go into nursing. And folks, thanks for feeding me a steady six-month diet of bull crap.

I slip on the sock and avoid Mom's gaze by fumbling with my shoe. She exchanges a worried look with Jac that I pretend not to see. Sighing, Mom finally makes her exit.

Jac breathes out. "Is it cold in here or is it just you?"

"I'm feeling rather toasty, actually." I finish tying the laces and give myself a once-over in the mirror. The sweater has to go.

"I can't believe you're mad at your dad for being sick."

"I'm not mad at him for being sick! I'm mad at them for lying. You should be able to relate to that."

"That's why? Really?"

No. Yes. That's part of it but . . . I don't know. "I don't want to talk about it," I say, throwing her my *drop it* look for added emphasis.

"So what's the big deal with visiting a counselor?" Jac taps her braces thoughtfully. "It gives you a little mystery. Guys love mystery."

I tug at the sweater, my muscular shoulders making it difficult to derobe gracefully. I finally succeed and throw the offensive item onto the cluttered floor. The static of the wool electrifies my frizzy brown hair. "Counselors are for crazies."

She points to my hair and grins. "Pumpkin, you iron your father's Dockers *for fun*. You were nuts long before this counselor came along."

23

"That's not crazy. It's cathartic."

"Cathartic? Isn't that, like, a laxative?"

"No, well yes, but that's not the definition I meant. I mean *catharsis*, an emotional purging."

"You just compared pressing pleats to diarrhea. You are crazy."

"Whatever." I slip a mustard yellow shirt off a hanger and hold it up. Jac snatches it and hands me a simple gray V-neck instead. I match. I think. "I haven't ironed in forever. And the only thing crazy about me is my choice in friends."

I love the girl to death, but it's true—Jac's certifiable, but in a far more purposeful way. Today she's wearing an eighties rock T-shirt with a Victorian skirt, orange suede clogs, and massive hoop earrings. Half of her long honey blond hair is braided while the other half flows free. It's not just her style. She uses random pet names for everyone, calling the postman sugar or the garbage guy lamb chop. Even her own name is bipolar—she's constantly switching between Jaclyn and Jac.

"What an honor." Jac hooks her arm through mine, guiding me out of the room and down the stairs. "Please don't forget us little people when they send you off to the psych ward."

I laugh, relieved I have Jac so I can joke about it with someone. And it really is funny that someone like me, someone appearing on every dean's list since preschool (okay, maybe preschools don't have a dean. But if they did . . .), has counseling appointments sandwiched between those of the school pyro and a notorious cheater.

My laughter stops once I'm in the kitchen. Trent, clad in scrub bottoms and an ancient Hooters shirt, leans against the counter, sipping a nauseating French coffee some desperate girl got him as a Christmas present. I grab an apple and hurry past, hoping to escape without conflict. I'm halfway out the door when I realize I've lost Jac, whose flirt radar is a twenty-four-hour marvel.

"So, how is swimming? You look like you've been practicing." Jac pours herself a cup of coffee and squeezes Trent's arm. "Or at least lifting weights."

"Jac." Trent scoots over. "Don't."

"But why?"

"You know it's illegal for me to flirt back."

"It's illegal for *Caleb* to flirt back," Jac says, like she's researched this thoroughly. Her crush on my brothers takes the "we could be sisters!" thing *way* too far. "He's twenty-three. But since you are still a teenager and I would totally consent—"

"Wouldn't happen. Even if you are cuter than any of the girls I ever went to high school with."

Jac squeals at the compliment. "But when I'm thirty you'll be thirty . . ."

She's crunching the numbers when my dad jogs in, drenched in sweat. "Morning, kids."

I choke on a piece of apple. I have his schedule timed now so I can avoid these awkward moments. This isn't fair. We have a routine. Well, he has a routine and I coordinate mine so they never overlap.

He opens the fridge and gulps orange juice directly from the carton. "You kids should come shoot around with me. I actually made a few this time. Guess you didn't want to get schooled before school, huh?"

At least Dad feels good enough today to exercise. That eases some of my anxiety.

Trent snorts and shakes his head. "Keep telling yourself that, Dad."

"So, Jac." Dad wipes his mouth on his sleeve. "Tell me how your first few weeks back from break are going. Still love high school?"

"No, Mr. Gritas. I've grown out of it."

"After one semester?"

"Yeah. I should just skip high school altogether, move on to college studies. College men. See, I'm really mature for my age—"

"Let's . . . let's go, Jac," I say.

Jac's lips settle into a practiced pout. "But I was finally wearing Trent down."

I abandon trying to give her the eye and focus on the hardwood floor. Dad's looking at me, I know it, looking at me with that what-happened-to-my-little-girl? look. Well, what happened is I grew up. And since he neglected to notice that, he thought it was okay to lie and protect me.

It's more than that, though. Not that I can really explain what the *more* is. All I know is that anytime I've seen either of my parents these last couple of weeks, I get a hot flash of mad. Which, of course, makes me feel awful. Then they'll do or say something and I stop feeling sorry and just feel . . . I don't know what it is. But it hurts.

It's pretty obvious why my calculated avoidance is easier. Why can't they give me some space? Eyes still focused on the ground, I grab Jac's hand. "Gotta go start my head research."

26

The door slams behind us. And I know it's impossible, but I can still feel my dad's eyes following me.

♥ ♥ ♥

I would be lying if I said I didn't get a kick out of the assignment. Here I am, a "troubled youth," and my self-chosen treatment is to become a stalker. Okay, not stalker. Research Analyst.

We race to school so I'll have some time to stake out Sean's locker. Jac's idea, of course. She's offered to aid in my mental healing because she has more experience when it comes to boys. As in, she's had experience—period. Boys are like Greek to me. Foreign.

"What's the rush?" I ask Jac once we're settled behind the large cement pillar about five feet from Sean's locker. "Why can't I just record my notes in biology?"

Jac blows a bang out of her face. "Pookie. You have to have fresh angles. Different lighting, different movement. And you can see the whole head, not just the back."

"Well, *I* better get started then," I say.

"What, you want me to leave? Fine. But make sure you see what's in his locker. You can tell a lot by what a guy has in his locker. It's like seeing into his soul." She does a double take as a boy walks by. "Look at that. Taj Langely. Holy mother, his shoulders are manly."

Jac leaves to pursue her own never-ending research of the male specimen, and I wait for Sean to get to school. Hmm. Funny, I don't even know how Sean gets to school.

Or where he lives.

Or who he lives with.

Or what he lives like.

Or what his likes *are*.

I guess I don't know Sean Griswold.

No. *Of course* I know Sean. I've known him for over seven years. He was the Tin Man and I was the Cowardly Lion in our fifth-grade production of *The Wizard of Oz*. When he threw up in seventh-grade math, it was on *my* favorite pair of sandals. The day after I lost the race for freshman class president, he turned around in biology and told me, "You're the better man, well, girl, for the job. Sorry you lost." I've lent the kid countless number two pencils and he's passed back limitless papers.

I can't remember school without Sean Griswold in it; yet I can't remember us ever having a real conversation.

Sean gets to his locker about five minutes before the morning bell. He carries a bike helmet under one arm and shoves it into his locker along with some weird-looking shoes. Taped inside the locker is a collage of cyclists. No pictures of skanky girls like most gorillas at this school. No cutouts of sports heroes. Just bike riders in neon spandex. He slams the locker shut before I can see more. I wait until his big blond head bobs around the corner and slide out my Focus Journal.

Payton's Focus Exercise AKA Sean Notes
January 18 7:58 AM
Topic: Bicycle Boy

1. Introduction
    A. Sean is either scared of aliens and wears
       a helmet to protect himself from getting

his brains sucked out or, more likely, he
rides a bike.

B. Another clue to that fact would be the
excessive array of cycling pictures
plastered in his locker. Where do you even
find pictures like that? <u>Dork Riders
Weekly</u>?

II. Body

  A. Bike riding is SO not cool

    1. Having your parents drop you off
is higher on the transportation
totem pole than having to lock up
your bike.

    2. Well, I guess it depends if you have
embarrassing parents or a beater car.

    3. No, doesn't matter. He carries
around a HELMET. Can't get lower
than that.

  B. Why bike riding?

    1. Is it because he won the school Bike
Rodeo in fourth grade and he's still
holding on to that moment of fame?

    2. Or is he nobly training to bike
across the country in order to
protest rising gas prices?

    3. Or does he simply hate walking?

III. Conclusion (Bringing it back to the almighty
head)

  A. So, something to know about Sean

Griswold's head: _It is safe as he pedals to and from school._

B. It's a wonder his hair still manages to look decent in third period with that obnoxious helmet flattening it out.

♥ ♥ ♥

School is out and the masses have dwindled. This is the time I love, hearing the solitary click of the principal's heels or the booming laughter drifting from Coach Berne's office. The staccato quiet is comforting, like the smell of lead from a box of number two pencils.

Except I'm not completely at peace. There's a nagging feeling I've forgotten something. I would check my lovely leather planner, but I can't remember where I put it, let alone the last time I wrote in it. Organization, coordination, concentration—basically all my former -ation skills—are all buried somewhere in my closet. Maybe it's a good thing I have my Focus Journal after all.

I thwonk my head against the cafeteria wall. Ouch. Why do people hit their head to get an idea? Zoning out is far more effective. I slide down to the ground and shift my attention to the JV swim guys hunched around a table in the back corner. Sean's there, big head and all. Should I write something? I know I'm staring but I can't stop. Is some blond hair and, if I'm being a little unscientific, a nice smile really going to help me remember all the things I'm forgetting? Even the things I want to forget?

Jac's play rehearsal should get out any minute. Maybe she'll remember whatever it is I've forgotten. This is pretty tragic when you consider I'm counting on the biggest airhead ever as my memory jogger. It once took me forty minutes to explain that Australia is both a continent and a country. The conversation concluded with her debating which Australian actor had the best abs.

My zoning ends when two of my former basketball team-mates, LaShelle and Rachel, burst through the cafeteria doors, laughing. They're wearing their maroon and silver team uniforms—the ones they wear to away games—with their hair in matching braids. Messy braids, I might add. I was the master braider on the team.

Basketball. I quit the day I got back from break. Midway through the season. I didn't even give a reason. Just walked into the coach's office and handed her my uniform. It was a few days after I Found Out. It seemed like a really logical move at the time, but all the reasons have settled into this blur. Dad coached me in basketball. He lied to me. And his ability to also play basketball, well... that could go away next relapse. The sport and my dad are so intertwined, just the look of my uni-form made me sick.

LaShelle and Rachel say something I can't hear to the swim-mers. Zach Hernandez, tall and untouchable, grabs the basket-ball Rachel's holding and dribbles around the tables. They're on the edge of the tile, right in front of the carpeted stairs, before she does a reach around and snatches her ball back.

"Foul!" Zach says.

"That was a steal!" Rachel turns back to LaShelle and the boys. "Was that a foul?"

LaShelle points at me. "Ask Gritas."

Rachel's braids whip her face. "Hey girl. Didn't see you there. Foul or not?"

"Oh." My cheeks burn. "I . . . I didn't see."

"Yes she did," Zach says. "She's covering for you. I get a free throw."

Rachel tosses the ball to Zach. "Take it."

I decide this is as good a time as any to examine the condition of my cuticles. They're ragged and in need of a good push down. I should do that now. In the bathroom. But Rachel stops me before I have a chance to save my cuticles. Or myself.

"Haven't seen you in a while," she says.

I force a smile. "Yeah. But I heard you guys beat Methacton."

"Barely." Rachel scratches her nose. "Could have killed them if you were still playing."

"Uh-huh."

Zach shoots the ball against the wall. The swimmers whistle.

"Wish you hadn't quit the team. I mean, you just kind of left without saying anything. And we're weak in the key now."

"Yeah, sorry." I look back at my nails. "Stuff came up."

"LaShelle said she heard your dad has cancer or something."

"Or something."

The ball rolls by us and Rachel swoops it up. "Take a pill, Zach. I'll bust you in a second." She bounces the ball under each leg, then hands it to me. "Hey, we've got a while before the bus comes. Wanna come warm up in the small gym?"

Yes. I want to warm up. I want to talk—really talk—with all my basketball friends again. I want to taste that need to push and drive and win. I cringe at every game announcement, every sneaker squeak, and especially every run-in with an old teammate, but I made my choice.

So please go away.

"I can't."

"It's cool. Well, I better go embarrass Zach. Adios, Gritas."

She sprints across the cafeteria and maneuvers around Zach before passing the ball to LaShelle. They call to the boys and skip out. Skip. When was the last time I skipped?

"Are you done already?" Jac asks. I jump. She's still wearing her *My Fair Lady* costume. At least I think it's her costume. You can never tell with Jac.

"Done with what?"

"Your Safety Council meeting."

I slap my forehead. That's it. "I forgot."

Jac plunks down next to me. "You forgot."

I nod.

Jac wiggles her fingers at the table of guys who, now that she's joined me, are looking our way. "Good luck at your meet, boys!" She lowers her voice. "Swimmers are the most underrated athletes. Just look at Trent and Caleb. Primo."

"Sick. I don't look at them like that. They're my brothers."

"What I wouldn't give to see them in a Speedo. Do you think Caleb's caught an accent now that he's in London? That'd be so hot."

"Accents aren't contagious."

"Fine, if I can't have your brothers, I'll take Zach. Or Sean."

She stares straight at him. I go back to analyzing my cuticles. "You know, even with the head, he's actually kind of cute. Hey, what did you find out this morning?"

"His head can't be too big because he managed to find a bike helmet that fits it. I am following a bicyclist." I look up from my cuticles and smile. "How weird is that?"

"Weird? Hello? Ever heard of Lance Armstrong, Mr. Hottie-Hot-Hot of sports? I bet Sean has killer calves. Can you see them under that table?" Jac licks her braces. "I might have to get myself a Focus Object too. Have any more cute heads I could follow?"

I give her a severe eye roll. Sean Griswold cute? This isn't about boy chasing. This is serious psychological research.

FIVE

Jac and I are halfway to her house when I tell her I'll call her later. Alone time is a must today. I walk slowly, kicking a rock along the sidewalk. At my street, I pick up the rock and throw it as far as I can and watch it bounce three times before stopping in Mr. Lopez's yard. He waves as he wipes down his red Camaro, just as he does every day, his breath visible in the chilly air. Usually, I'd go over and talk to him, but today I just nod and slip through our back gate.

All I have to do now is sneak through the back door and tiptoe up the stairs without my mom hearing—

"Payton, is that you?"

She was waiting. Ever since she quit her part-time job as an art curator at a gallery downtown, exercising and waiting—for me to get home, for Trent to go back to school, for Dad to get better—is all she ever does.

"No," I yell.

"Come into the living room and talk to me."

I make a desperate dash for my room. I'm almost home free when Trent blocks my door.

"Move." I look behind my shoulder to make sure Mom hasn't followed me.

"Make me."

"You know I can't do that. Look, I'm not in the mood, got it?"

Trent raises a waxed eyebrow. Yes, I'm related to a male eyebrow waxer who, surprisingly, is Very Much Straight. He started waxing his eyebrows after he shaved his legs, which was after the Nair-on-the-chest debacle. He's a swimmer, that's his excuse, but come on—is extra eyebrow hair really going to slow you down in the water?

"The mood? The mood to what?" he asks. "Hang out with your family? Talk to Mom?"

"No. I'm not in the mood to deal with my nosy brother who should be off at college so I can finally live my dream of being an only child."

"Well, someone has to hang around to help Dad. Now that you've peaced out on him."

"I have not peaced . . . Will you just move. Please?"

Trent shrugs and moves out of the doorway. "I didn't realize fifteen-year-olds have such busy schedules."

"And I didn't realize college kids have no lives!" I shout before slamming my door.

I flop onto my bed and stare at the ceiling. Trent didn't used to annoy me so much. I was actually glad when he decided to transfer from Penn State to the local community college for a year. He said it was so he could make extra money selling pest control and I bought it. Not the pest control—the lie. It wasn't until recently that I discovered his real reason for moving home was my dad.

Trent did at least tell me this: After Dad's MRI, my parents sat down with my brothers and talked all about the disease. Trent insisted he move home for a year, putting his swimming scholarship on hold, putting his life on hold. I don't know what difference he thought his presence would make, like the family couldn't survive without his hair removal tips and annoying music. Like he could make Dad get better. They said no, but he still showed up last August anyway.

I'm sure the only idea everyone agreed upon was to shield little, naive Payton from the Big MS Monster. Which is total bs. I mean, I'm old enough to go to PG-13 movies. In some cultures I can even be *married*. Not to mention my already proven track record of responsibility and civil service. It's ridiculous that my family thought I was the only one too immature to know that my dad has a disease.

Even worse, Dad claims his disease doesn't change any- thing. What *doesn't* it change?

What I know about my dad's MS is that it's at a stage where he can relapse at any time. It's actually one of the better stages, because it's not a continual decline. He'll go weeks or months with nothing wrong and then relapse and go numb again. Dur- ing his worst relapse, the numbness spread from just his hand to his entire left side. Sometimes the numbness affects his sense of touch, so he can't feel anything, like his hand is asleep. But occasionally, it's like his brain can't tell his fingers what they want them to do. His job as a dentist relies on the ability to work on small things with his hands. Mom said if things get really bad, he can always find a job teaching. Yeah. Like *that's* reassuring.

I mean, it isn't cancer. It . . . people don't . . . necessarily die. Don't do chemo. They don't follow a set recovery plan. They just change. Their body changes. Their abilities—the things they do that make them who they are—leave, sometimes temporarily, sometimes forever. Every day they wake up with that big *what if?*

And nothing is scarier than a life filled with *what ifs*—living day by day without predictability and control. Some people end up losing feeling. Some have uncontrollable spasms. Some can't function. Some end up blind or in a wheelchair. Some end up bedridden and paralyzed.

It's hard to know who "some people" will be.

♥ ♥ ♥

I fall asleep thinking about Dad and my first day of Field Research, but wake up about a half hour later when I hear a basketball bouncing outside. I peep through the blinds. Dad's home early, working on his free throws.

He misses three in a row, bounces the ball and pauses, consumed by concentration. Even from a distance, I can see the ball shaking. Next shot, the ball circles the rim twice before bouncing out. Dad jumps up to get the rebound, but when he comes down, he freezes. I can only see his face in profile, but he looks horrified. A few moments later, I notice the water he is standing in. I'm confused at first—it hasn't rained; I don't get where it came from. Then I see the front of his sweats and . . . oh my gosh . . . my dad . . . wet himself. A grown man. I'm sure the expression on my face matches his horror.

Healthy people don't lose control of their bladder from one little jump. This is so not fine. So not.

He bends over, hands on his knees, shaking his head. I knew incontinence was an MS symptom, but knowing it's possible and actually *watching* my dad pee his pants is something else entirely. I'm so embarrassed, so embarrassed for him, that I can't watch anymore. I snap the blinds shut and sink into my computer chair. My phone is lit with three texts from Jac. I consider ignoring her and resuming my much-needed nap, but ignoring Jac is about as easy as ignoring a zit on your nose. Besides, I need something to erase that image of my dad right now. Uck.

> **Jaclyn:** Hey, what R U doing?
> **Jaclyn:** Hell-ooooooooooooooo?
> **Jaclyn:** I know U R there. Fine, if U don't want to know what I found out about Sean, your loss. Here I am, trying to be a good friend and U can't even get off your butt and come see what I have to say
> **Payton Gritas:** I'm here
> **Jaclyn:** Oh. I knew U were. Here, I'll call U
> **Payton Gritas:** No, I'm having my alone time, remember?
> **Jaclyn:** U R so drama
> **Payton Gritas:** Tell me quick
> **Jaclyn:** Sean Griswold's mom is a real estate queen. I did a search on his name and her website came up—she mentioned Sean on the bio part of her site. Anyway, check it out

Payton Gritas: What's the site?

Jaclyn: I'll e-mail you the link. They must be loaded. Seriously loaded. Do U know where he lives?

Payton Gritas: No

Jaclyn: U R not a very good stalker then

Payton Gritas: RESEARCH ANALYST

Jaclyn: What does that even mean?

Payton Gritas: I don't know. It just sounds good. Look, I just started TODAY! Stop doing my job

Jaclyn: Sheesh. U R welcome, babycakes

Payton Gritas: Thank you. I owe you my life. Where would I be without your ingenious internet savvy?

Jaclyn: Shut up

Payton Gritas: Shutting. Checking link. Late

Jaclyn: XOXO

I'm clicking on the link when there's a knock on the door.

"I'm busy," I call. Despite the Big MS Lie, I'm talking to my parents. I just limit all correspondence to two or three syllables. I only hope it's my mom and not . . .

My dad pushes the door open. "Hey, sunshine. What are you doing?"

I close out the open links and turn my body so I'm blocking the screen. "Nothing." I can't look him in the eye. He's show-ered and changed his clothes. I wonder if he told Mom or did the laundry himself.

"Studying for midterms?"

"Sure." One syllable. Safe.

"Too bad. I was just shooting around outside."

No mention of his accident. That's good. I can ignore it too. "Oh."

"Hey." He fiddles with the strings on his hoodie. "I was thinking we should go down to the city tonight. Maybe get some Geno's steaks. I won't even gag when you put Cheez Whiz on yours." He smiles.

My dad's smile is more infectious than a yawn. He'll smile at a total stranger, and even in downtown Philadelphia people smile back. Then again, they might just smile out of fear—the man is well over six feet tall with hair covering his whole body from the neck down. His head is just as noticeable as Sean's, not because of the hair but the lack thereof. So when he smiles, it's like a mutant-sized baby is cooing at you. A baby with lots of fur.

I smile back for a moment but turn the corners of my mouth down. "Not hungry." One, two, three.

"Not hungry for Geno's trademarked gut bomb? Is it even possible?" Dad folds his arms and leans against the side of my computer desk. "Okay. Maybe another time. How's everything else going? Was school good today?"

School. I forget about his basketball playing and brush a stray bang away from my face. I want to say, *The stupid counselor you are torturing me with unknowingly assigned me to analytically research a guy I've known since grade school. All because you never told me there was something wrong with you.* But I don't. Instead, I shrug.

"Come on, let's gut bomb it. Or at least come shoot around with me."

I stare at my computer screen and open a bunch of random documents. Is he serious? Doesn't he remember what he just did fifteen minutes ago? What if I had been shooting around with him then? "Sorry," I answer. Even without my syllable rule, I doubt I can say any more to him right now. "Homework."

"All right. I'm just . . . I'm trying to make this right. I really am. I hope you can . . ." Dad's voice trails off into a cough used to disguise his hurt. My eyes stay glued on the computer screen until he leaves.

When he does, I let out a sigh, hoping it releases some of the bad karma I just incurred from being so heinous. I don't want to be like this, but I don't know how else I'm supposed to act. Like nothing is wrong? Like he didn't just pee his pants?

One of my desk drawers is open, and I'm about to slam it shut when I pause to admire the order inside. At least everything is mostly in its proper storage compartments there. At least *that* part of my life is still together.

I open a box of pictures and thumb back to my last batch of digitals I'd printed off before . . . before all this. There's a picture of my dad in his old 76ers T-shirt and blinding smile, handing me a poorly wrapped basketball. And me, feigning surprise. "A basketball, Dad! I'd never have guessed."

I own twelve basketballs. Dad has gotten me one every year since I was three—all colors, all sizes. The balls, just like the sport, were our bond. I used to display them on a shelf in my room. They're in the garage now.

I rub the picture between my fingers, and for a split second consider ripping it, but instead shove it back in the box. I check that my door is still shut, then kneel down and rummage under my bed until I find what I'm looking for.

My dad's old Sixers shirt. I know he'd combed the house looking for it, but I'd taken it out of the laundry the last time he wore it. It smelled like him, like Old Spice deodorant and toothpaste and that Christmas morning when everything was so perfect and yet completely not, and every morning and every day I had with him before MS.

I'd started sleeping with it under my pillow. I don't know why. I know it's weird and probably creepy treating an old shirt as a teddy bear. Maybe my stalker tendencies were stronger than I thought. But it helps me fall asleep, and it's there when I wake up crying in the middle of the night.

PFE
January 25
Topic: A Flow Chart on Sean's Head

Sean seems like a pretty clean guy
↓
Meaning, he's always decently dressed
(he matches, his clothes aren't stained
and fit him well)
↓
And he smells good, so he obviously bathes
↓
Or showers. No fifteen-year-old guys bathe
↓
And his nails are trimmed and his hair's cut
and styled too

Why are there random hairs growing on his
neck like dandelions in sidewalk cracks?

↓

It makes no sense that a guy who thinks to
wear deodorant and clip his fingernails is
unaware of neck hair

↓

How does it not bother him?

↓

Shave it, Sean! Pay a visit to your barber

↓

If not for you, then for everyone
who spends at least one period a day
systematically investigating your head

♥ ♥ ♥

Jac's mom is just leaving when I arrive for our Saturday
sleepover. After pausing for the customary compliment, this
time on her turquoise dress exhibiting cleavage bigger than
Sean's head, she mentions to Jac that she might be crashing
at a "friend's" house. This from the woman who used to wear
Christmas sweater vests and serve mini sausages at Parents
Against Profanity meetings. But that was before her husband
traded her in for his office assistant, who Jac knew pretty well
because she used to babysit Jac. Back when the assistant/
girlfriend was in high school. Which was, like, six years ago.

"You like my mom's new Botox fix?" Jac asks as we pass through the hideously ornate house, a bronzed fairy leering at us as we go.

"It wasn't bad," I lie.

"Whatever. It makes Joan Rivers look natural." She snorts. "Let's get on the computer. I feel like doing some self-Googling. I just hope Mom hasn't posted pictures of me again calling me her little sister. I'll die."

Jac leads me into her safari-themed room complete with a zebra wall, lit candles, and exotic pillows thrown around her canopied bed. I blow out the tiny flames and turn on the ostrich-feathered lamp instead. Jac's always wanted to date a firefighter. If she keeps those candles burning, she might just get her wish.

We've transitioned out of most of our childhood rituals, but for some reason the sleepovers have stuck. Sometimes we'll include a few girls from our various circles, but introducing other people can be risky. In seventh grade, Cailee Murphy brought some nasty vodka and Jac drank most of it before wobbling out to the living room to yell at her dad. Who, of course, wasn't there. I don't know what I am capable of being peer-pressured into after the week I've had, so I'm relieved it's just Jac and me tonight. We can be silly and stupid and not care.

"That shirt is huge on you." Jack nods at my dad's Sixers shirt that I've now taken to wearing as pajamas.

"Oh. It's comfy."

"Isn't that your dad's?"

"Yeah. I just grabbed it on my way out. I need to do laundry."

"You could wear one of my shirts if you want."

45

"Um . . . I'm good." I shrug.

Jac nods knowingly. "I used to wear my dad's shirts after . . ."

The end of the sentence hangs in the air and we both look away.

"Computer?" she asks.

I breathe a sigh of relief. "Good idea."

We order some takeout and spend the better part of the night looking up ourselves and everyone we know, getting lost in the chain the Internet creates. Our best find—a guy with my same name is wanted in three states. We think it's so hilarious that the next morning we download a picture of me and spend the rest of the day figuring out how to merge pictures together so we could put my face on a prisoner's body. I look fabulous as a three-hundred-pound Hungarian man.

Then Jac gets the idea to do the same thing to a picture of Sean. We look up his mom's website again, scrolling down to the "Family First" section. There's a photo of Sean from about fourth grade, the year after we first had him in our class. He's sitting on a beach with the sunlight behind him, grinning as he holds up a large seashell.

"Whoa, look at that thing," Jac says.

"Yeah, it's a big shell."

"Not the shell. That huge cut on his head. Have you ever noticed it before?"

I squint at the computer screen. Sure enough, there is a jagged wound running down his left temple. Hello, big gaping hole in my research. How did I not notice that? "That's weird. I don't remember him having a cut that bad. You'd think we'd remember that. Wonder what happened."

46

"It looks like someone sliced him open. Maybe he got knifed."

"How many fourth graders get knifed?" I ask.

Jac shrugs. "Remember, we don't really know him. He could be a gangbanger. Or a spy."

"Or he could have fallen off his bike."

Jac taps the screen with her green lacquered fingernail. "Well, we're going to find out what happened. It's bound to be a good story."

"What, you're going to Google fourth-grade knifings?"

"No." Jac picks up the phone. "I'm just going to call him and ask."

SIX

I lunge for the phone. "You are NOT calling Sean Griswold! You don't even know his number."

"Lollipop." Jac hides the phone behind her back. "This is for you. Penetrating investigative research requires a leap out of our comfort zones."

"My comfort zone is research analyst. *You're* leaping into stalker status."

She clicks the mouse. "Look, there's his phone number. It's a sign. And who are we to defy a cosmic sign?"

"First off, this is *my* assignment. And second, I'm supposed to be writing about his head, not calling him on the phone."

"Right." Jac punches in the number. "His head, which is messed up in the picture and we are about to find out why."

I grab for the phone again but before I can stop her, someone picks up the other line.

"Hi. Is Sean there?" Pause. "Do you know where he is?" Longer pause. "This is a friend of his. We go way back. But no message. Thanks."

Relief floods over me and I burst into giggles. He isn't there. He isn't going to find out about my Focus Journal. "You go way back?"

Jac starts giggling too. Every time we try to say something, we look at each other and laugh more, until we're not so much laughing at the phone call as we are just laughing to laugh.

Jac finally flops down on her bed, her hair spraying across the many pillows. Her pink strappy tank top and retro-print skirt clash beautifully with the olive bedspread. "Third grade *is* way back."

"Oh, yeah. You two are soul mates."

"What was I supposed to say? I don't know who I just talked to, but he was weird. Started to tell me Sean was at the movies, then got all secretive and began asking questions."

"Well, it was probably his dad. That's how dads are."

"Maybe. Or a cousin. Or a fellow gang member, or . . . Who else could it be?"

I shrug. "You're asking me? How would I know?"

"Well, if you were a good stalker—"

"I'm not a—"

"Fine. If you were a good"—she does air quotes with her fingers—"'Research Analyst' you would. Anyway, I'm going to figure out that huge scar mystery soon, and then I want to know who that crusty guy I just talked to is." Jac twists a braid around her finger. "And I wonder what kind of movies Sean likes?"

"Why does that matter?"

"Wrong question. This is fun. So why not?"

"Maybe we're taking it too far. I'm just keeping a stupid journal about his head. I don't need to know the rest of this stuff."

"Really? I think you do." Jac rolls out of her bed and crawls back over to the computer. "Like, a scientist starts with a hypothesis, right?"

"Yeah."

"But their findings and experiments can take them in a whole new direction. They start off asking why snakes have scales and end up finding a cure for cancer!"

"That's the dumbest thing I've ever heard."

"You're limiting yourself, that's all I'm saying. You have a mighty fine specimen with tons of research potential. Branch out. Start with the cut."

I glance at the clock and shoot up. "Crap. I've got to study for my algebra midterm."

"You . . . you aren't ready?"

I avert my eyes. It's a first, for sure. "Technically . . . no. But it'll be fine. I'd better call Trent to pick me up. I'll figure out what to do with the Sean stuff. And Jac?"

Jac looks up from the website photo. "Yeah?"

"Promise me no more phone calls."

Jac lets out a theatrical sigh. "You really are taking all the drama out of this."

♥ ♥ ♥

Trent picks me up, but only after Jac spends a good five minutes flirting with him. Trent even goes along with it to humor her. At least I hope that's the reason. The alternative is too disgusting to imagine.

Trent sings along with his punk music as we drive home,

50

a clear indicator he's in a good, nonconfrontational mood. I relax and even join in on the lines I know, which isn't hard because it's mostly just repeated, angst-ridden rants against society. I secretly agree with some of the punk theology, although I don't know how following the anarchist trend is possible. Following any sort of establishment goes against the very definition of anarchy. I'm trying in vain to explain this to Trent when he stops the car in the driveway and sighs.

"Payton. When are you going to start acting your age?"

"What do you mean?"

"You just used the words *theology* and *angst-ridden* to describe music."

"That's not music."

"Well, you should be like, Wow, this totally rocks! or something less . . . less . . ."

"Intelligent?"

"Exactly. No." He pauses. "Just more teenagerish."

"I did teenagerish things all weekend, whatever that means."

"Like what? Discuss global warming?"

"No, even though I should point out global warming is not an age-specific concern. Everyone, young and old, has to share this planet and—"

"See."

"All right. Teenagerish. We did hair. Ate junk. Stalked boys."

"My sister a stalker? Doubt it."

I bristle. "What's that supposed to mean?"

"Well, you don't exactly walk on the wild side. This stuff with Mom and Dad is the most rebellious I've seen you. Caleb didn't believe me when I told him you weren't talking to them."

"What does Caleb know about me anyway? He lives on the other side of the world."

"And before that he lived in the same house as you, and even if he didn't, everyone knows you're totally straight edge."

"No way! I do outrageous things."

"Like what?"

My mind goes blank. "One time I wore mismatched socks to school for a whole day."

Trent throws back his head and laughs.

"On purpose!" I add. "Someone has to be good after the reputations you and Caleb had."

Trent dries his eyes on the collar of his shirt. "True. You're the glue. That's why Dad—"

I open the car door before he can make me feel any worse. "I gotta start studying. Night."

But I don't get much studying done. Instead, I log back onto Sean's mom's site and stare at a beaming Sean. I go to bed with the same question that has been bugging me for days—how can you go so long knowing someone without really *knowing* them at all?

Payton's Focus Exercise AKA PFE
January 28 Right before the departure bell
Topic: A brief review of last week's Sean findings

**Note: After much scientific consideration (and encouragement from Jac), I've decided to expand upon my head research and include the rest of Sean in my exercises. For science's sake.

K–W–L Chart

(K) What do I know?	(W) What do I want to know?	(L) What have I learned?
He's a pill popper. Not like, drugs or anything, but he eats Advil like candy.	So what's with the pills? Does his neck hurt from the strain of holding up his head?	Well, everything in the K category.
He has a weird scar on his forehead.	Where did he get that scar? Why didn't I notice it before?	And then I guess I can fill this in later after I conquer the W.
I have his schedule pretty nailed down now.	Where does he go after fifth period? I mean, I was right behind him in the hall, and he just disappeared. We were over by the Hall of Terror, which he wouldn't have gone into, so maybe he just slipped into a bathroom.	You know what? This one's a stupid graphic organizer.

SEVEN

Midterms—an overview.

1. My highlighting system saves me in English.
2. Reasoning and guessing get me through algebra.
3. I'm not sure about the multiple choice in history, but I compared everything to Modern America on the essays. Can't go wrong with that.
4. We do a word search in health. God bless whoever schlepped Coach Essary through college.
5. *Español es muy simpatico.* Especially since my mom is always speaking it under her breath. Although those words did not appear on the test.
6. Biology. There are questions from the videos. Unfortunately for me, there is not one question about Sean's head.

♥ ♥ ♥

We interrupt your regularly scheduled
programming to broadcast this news:

Sean Cut His Hair
- No more neck hair!
- It's kind of spiky—makes him look older.
- And somehow, his head looks smaller.
  Maybe all that "bigness" was the work of
  voluminizing shampoo.
- His scar is SO clear. How did I not notice
  it before?

Miss Marietta always returns papers by having the first person in the row pass them back, which is beyond unfair because then everyone who sits in front of you can see your grade. Usually it's fine, but it's the written part of our midterm, which I bombed. I don't need my early-teens crisis broadcast to my whole row.

Sean turns around to hand me the papers and I stare at the scar on the top left edge of his forehead. It's how the last week has played out, actually. Ever since Jac and I saw that picture, the scar has become the focus within my focus. It's so notice-able now—raised with a pinkish tinge.

Jac's been pushing me to ask Sean what happened, until finally I promised to do it today. She has all these scar theories she thinks I should add to my findings, but I like to think my Focus Journal is honest journalism, not the *National Enquirer* equivalent, so I'm not going to include her "Had one lobe of his brain removed" hypothesis to my notes.

Anyway, Sean hands me the papers, then leans over to Spencer Lund to say something. And it's like a window of opportunity is closing, like not finding out about his scar will bring a standstill to my research. I'm starting to enjoy my research. I haven't even done a pie chart yet.

So I tap Sean on the shoulder and he glances back at me.

At this point, I have no plan. I avoid the scar by looking at his eyes, which I notice aren't really brown like I'd originally thought, but almost gold with a brown rim. I should add that to my notes. By now, I've been staring at him for five seconds and his eyebrows are up in a question. So I blurt out the first thing I can think of to say.

"I just got a paper cut. From those papers you passed back." Liar. I grab my right pointer finger and suck on it.

"Oh. Sorry about that," Sean says.

"It's just, I really hate cuts, don't you? Paper cuts aren't a big deal, but I've had some nasty cuts before. Like, I had to get stitches on my knee once and it stung for weeks. Have you ever had a cut like that before?"

Sean's eyebrows remain arched, but now they've moved from a question to surprise. I never talk to Sean. He never talks to me. Well, we might say hi or bye or little flickers of small talk, but I've never gone off like I just did. My research has reached a new level. As his eyebrows go back down, the corners of his mouth curve up.

"Yeah, I've had a cut like that before."

"Really?"

"Sure. You're right. They suck." And he turns back around.

What was I expecting? A heartfelt retelling of how he got the thing? That we'd suddenly be bonded by flesh wounds?

I crumple up my test without looking at it. I'm sure I failed, just like I'm failing with my Focus Object. Now, if it were Jac, she'd march right up to Sean and ask without hesitation, "So, what's with that scar?"

I hope she doesn't try to "help" like that. Not that I'm into him—it's just that her meddling could really contaminate my findings.

♥ ♥ ♥

So much for that hope. Jac spends our whole lunch yapping about Sean. Maybe I should have written about the pencil sharpener after all.

"I saw him today. That haircut is smoking hot. And you can see his scar better, which gives him kind of a bad-boy look, don't you think?"

"No."

"Did you find out where he got it?"

Jac and I have been friends since the world started turning. And I never lie to her. Well, not big lies. Last week, I did say her purple boots were cute over her jeans, but that was only because I really wanted to leave and she'd already changed a gazillion times. I should have told her about the conversation with Sean but something was holding me back.

"Yeah, I asked him." I nibble on a french fry. "I was right. Fell off his bike. Nothing noteworthy."

Disappointment clouds her face as she plays with the tab on her Coke can. "Well, that's not very fun. I thought for sure there was some kind of weapon involved. So you really talked to him?"

"I said I did."

"Maybe this assignment will be good for you after all. You never talk to people you don't know well. I'm proud of you, pumpkin." Jac wipes a fake tear from her eye. "My little girl is coming out of her shell."

What I really want to do is crawl into a hole. She's only trying to help—just because she turns everything else into the Jac Show doesn't mean she'll do it with this. "Hey, I still don't know where he goes in between fifth and sixth period. Want to be my assistant analyst?"

Jac puts her hand over her heart. "I would be honored. Maybe we'll find something scandalous after all."

"Uh . . . maybe," I say. Like someone as normal as Sean Griswold could be scandalous. Honestly.

♥   ♥   ♥

Jac is waiting outside of my class when the fifth period bell rings. I don't bother to ask how she got there so fast. Probably embarrassed Mr. Boyle with an excuse about female problems. She wears a long trench coat and black sunglasses. I already regret asking her for help.

"Where did you get the outfit?" I ask.

"This guy last period had it on and I told him he could copy my homework if I borrowed it. Very James Bond, right?"

58

"It smells funny."

"Just adds to the authenticity."

I spot Sean across the quad, skirting around the cheer-leaders, walking with his shoulders slightly hunched. It's not an insecure, Charlie Brown–style walk, but more like he's an island. Not unreachable, not deserted, but still alone. "There's Sean. We have to be quick. Can you take those glasses off so you can actually see him? I don't want to lose him again."

Jac salutes me and hitches up the collar of her coat. "The sunglasses stay. Just call me the chameleon."

I grab her hand and weave through the crowded quad until we're a few feet behind Sean. We follow him through the cafe-teria, a shortcut to the west wing of the school.

Field Research is tough work, especially with the baggage. Jac lowers her sunglasses at every boy who cruises by, catcalling and purring. When a gangly senior reciprocates her advances with a head nod, she stops completely to flirt. I nudge, then push. "Sorry," she calls to her admirer. "Top-secret assignment!"

Sean pauses in front of a hallway and looks behind his back. Jac and I both point to the wall and loudly discuss the history of the Spirit of '76 mural. He disappears and we're about to follow him when I realize where he's gone.

"He's going into the Hall of Terror!" I say, grabbing Jac's arm to stop her.

"I know. How cool. And I'm totally going to blend in with this trench coat." She turns around the corner and since my hand is still on her arm, I involuntarily follow.

Involuntary is putting it mildly. I swore I'd never come back here.

The Hall of Terror is the hallway where the halogen lights burn out sooner than they should. Some say ghosts of past students drink from the water fountain. It is also where the Goths/Druggies/Freaks hang out.

If you have a locker in this hallway, you switch with someone ASAP. Sure, they'll know your locker combo, but people that fried can't even remember their own name, so who cares? Not that I'm trying to regurgitate Modern American high school stereotypes. I'm sure the unsavories have feelings too. Artificial feelings resulting from abusing illegal substances, but feelings nonetheless.

Okay, I am biased, but here's the reason. I had a locker in this hallway at the beginning of the year. It was close to most of my classes, so I declined the two offers to switch. One day, while I was getting my books out of my locker, the looks-like-he's-twenty-and-probably-is junior with the locker above me leaned down and said, "Those among the living should not walk among the dead." Then, he BIT me. Seriously, like a vampire—although this was more like a nibble on my shoulder. A warning. I was so freaked out that I didn't even care when my new locker was across the school. Better to be late to class than risk a vampire hickey.

"Stop!" I finally get out, my shoulder aching from the memory. "We can't go in the hallway. It'll look . . . suspicious."

"Suspicious?"

My brain works fast. If she knows I'm simply scared, she'll drag me down the hallway just to help me overcome my fear. "Yeah. We have to be stealth. Let's peek around the corner instead."

We squeeze behind the wall so we have a better view of the people coming and going. The hairs on my arms stand at attention as each person walks by, but Jac just smiles at all the future criminals.

"Hey, look," she says. "He's talking to someone."

I stick my head out from behind the corner and survey the hall. I spot Sean standing by my old locker talking to a guy whose back is to us. The guy says something and Sean laughs. Laughter seems out of place in the Hall of Terror, but for some reason Sean does not. He sticks out appearance-wise with his hair, crisp polo, and Adidas sneakers. But everybody that walks by is oblivious to him, like he's just another school ghost.

"Well, we better get to class," I say. "Mystery solved."

The other guy takes something out of his backpack and shakes it before handing it to Sean. I can't tell what it is, but it looks like a pill bottle. I'm about to duck back around the corner when Sean makes eye contact with me. I freeze and stare back. He gives me the same bemused look I got in biology when I rambled on about cuts. He mumbles something to the guy in front of him, who also turns around. The guy's face, dominated by a mushroom-shaped nose and watery eyes, breaks into a smile. Either that or he's flashing his fangs. Vampire Boy.

"What's wrong?" Jac asks. "You look like you've seen a ghost."

I dodge around the corner and take off. I am not willing to risk my neck, or my life, in the name of therapeutic research.

EIGHT

PFE
February 1—After school
Topic: Questions

1. Why is someone like Sean Griswold hanging out in the Hall of Terror with the kid who almost sucked the life out of me?
2. Why is it that the more I find out about this guy, the more I'm totally baffled by him?
3. Why is Jac going psychotic over this whole thing and insisting I talk to Sean ASAP?
4. And why do I have this weird desire to branch out in my research and do exactly what she suggests?

My mom is not a crier. She's not incapable of crying. She cried when my oldest brother left for college and she cried when she fell down the stairs and broke her leg in three places. But she's not one to get weepy during a movie. I had never even seen her cry about the Dad thing. Which is why I'm worried to see her sprawled out on the couch in the middle of the day, inhaling a can of mixed nuts and bawling her eyes out. Is it a really good *Oprah* rerun, or is Dad getting worse?

"Mom?" I close the door softly behind me.

Mom sniffs and wipes her eyes. She's still in her workout clothes from this morning. "Oh. Hey. I didn't hear you come home."

Maybe I should talk to her. I haven't really *talked* to her in weeks. She seems so depressed. It makes me wonder if she was like this for the last few months and I just didn't notice. And why wouldn't she be? Dad and Mom are soul mates. They met back in college, at Penn. Dad was going to dental school and Mom was an art history major from Arizona. Dad was cleaning her teeth and asked her what she liked to eat—his not-smooth way of asking her out. She thought he was commenting on her breath and got offended. But not too offended, because they got married three years later. I guess even oral hygiene can be romantic in the right setting.

And now he's sick. I'm almost willing to give in a bit to perk Mom up. *Almost.*

"I just talked to Caleb," Mom continues. "He's having a hard time being so far away while things are . . . he's just having a tough time."

"Oh."

"He said to tell you hi."

Hi. You're eight years older than me and I hardly know you

63

and you get to go to school in freaking London and hang out with cool British scholars and stay away from the drama and then complain about it while I get to suffer here. Hi.

"You hungry?" Mom asks.

I drop my backpack on the ground and kind of smile. "Gyros?"

"Really?" Mom props herself up on her elbows. "Like from the mall food court? That's a great idea. Let's wait until Trent and Dad get home and we'll all go together as a family. Maybe we could talk about what we're going to do for spring break."

See, this is why you never give in to parents. I'm thinking a little step like gyros, and she's going for a bomb like spring break. "I don't—"

"I'm just going to go freshen up." Mom's eyes shine. "We haven't done something as a family since . . . well, in a while."

Since I found out you're all liars? I bite my tongue. This is my own doing. If Vampire Boy doesn't kill me, family bonding will.

♥ ♥ ♥

Two hours later, my family is getting their bond on in the King of Prussia mall. The plus side of Mom's enthusiasm is she's also eager to buy me some new clothes. The downside is everyone tries way too hard to act like hanging out is normal and not a Very Big Step toward mending our family's battered group dynamic. Ms. Callahan's words, not mine.

Somehow, I find myself in a dressing room trying on bathing suits for my mom. I try to argue, but she's riding this buzz

I can't kill. She keeps talking about the spring break trip she wants our family to take, even though we've never gone all together. It's driving me nuts.

Although doctors don't know exactly what causes MS, they do know that there are factors that may bring on a relapse. The doctor said that heat is a trigger for my dad, which may be why he had his first occurrence in Cancun. Last spring break. So really, our family should be moving to Antarctica, not planning a beach party IN THE SUN.

And I'm the one in denial.

Mom gives up on the wild Hawaiian-print bikinis she's been flinging over the dressing room and hands me a black one-piece with a halter neck.

"Do you have it on?" Mom asks.

I look at my butt in the mirror. There are two looks in our family. My dad's a Euro-mutt: Greek, Spanish, and Swiss. So my brothers have these cool blue eyes with strong jaws reeking of alpha maleness. Then there's me, straight from the Colombian side: ample butt and enough body hair that my mom let me shave my legs in the fourth grade. At least I got her waist and skin that looks like it's perma-tan, both qualities set off in the suit. But the body hair—genetic joke. "It's not me."

Mom yanks the door open and peers inside. "What? You're beautiful! That's the best I've ever seen you look. In anything."

"Stop it." I cover up the low neckline.

Mom shakes her head. "Wait until spring break. Your father will have a heart attack."

"That's if he doesn't have an MS attack first," I say under my breath.

"What's that?"

The heart attack line reminds me that, despite the tears earlier and the overall happy tone, I'm still generally pissed. Who I'm mad at or why I'm mad all melt into one sizzling eruption. *I don't like the suit, okay? Gosh, it's nearly ten degrees outside and you have me in here trying on bathing suits, which by the way only adds to the objectification of women.*

"I hate this," I snap.

Mom flinches, then her eyes glaze over. "Let's go find the boys."

We don't say a word as we leave the store and step onto the escalator. The buzz of nearby shoppers only deepens the tension I've once again managed to create. I would say I'm sorry, but I'm not. I mean, I *am* sorry that I can't really communicate whatever it is I'm feeling, but an apology doesn't change that my mom's planning a trip that I don't think should happen.

Trent and my dad are in the Gap, stocking up on a mountain of boxer briefs. Unlike me, Trent is using the peppy parental mood to his full advantage.

"Isn't it weird to underwear shop with your family?" I ask Trent.

"Feeling left out, little sis? Want to go pick up a training bra?"

I turn to my dad in a huff. "Dad!"

He ignores the argument and holds a pink miniskirt against his waist. "Is it me?"

I roll my eyes and snatch it from him. "It's more Trent."

"I think you're right." Trent grabs the skirt in a larger size and squeezes his skinny butt right into it. He looks better in it than I would, a fact almost as tragic as seeing my brother in drag.

A salesclerk frowns at Trent, who's now sashaying around the store. Mom and Dad burst into a fit of giggles. Well, she couldn't have been too hurt by what I said if she's laughing again. I bury my face into a flannel shirt and count to ten slowly before taking a peek to see if the humiliation is over.

It isn't. Standing in front of me is Sean Griswold. And he's not smiling.

"Hey," I say, because what else would I say?

"Hey. What are you doing?"

"Hiding from family." I point to Trent, who is now dancing with a mannequin while my parents hold their stomachs, laughing.

A hint of a smile tugs on the corners of Sean's mouth. "He's a natural."

"Yeah, well, we're hoping he moves to New York soon and makes it big. Everyone needs a dream, I guess."

Sean nods. We stand there in silence, watching as the saleslady finally asks Trent to remove the skirt and leave the mannequin alone.

"So, what's up with you?" Sean asks, back to his darker mood.

"Nothing. Just hanging out with my family."

"No. I mean . . ." Sean lets out a breath. "Look, I got this weird phone call today from some girl trying to make her voice deep. She told me to meet her at the mall by the gyro place at six and that she'd be wearing a red shirt."

I look down to assess my outfit. Sure enough, my shirt is the predicted color.

"So I come, I don't know why. I don't get many calls like that, so I'm curious. And then I see you sitting there with your family but you don't even see me. And the weird thing is I seem to be seeing a lot of you lately. More than usual. I guess we see each other every day, but every time I turn around in the halls, you're there. So what gives?"

I have no doubt that my face matches my shirt. It's hard for me to answer Sean because I'm too busy planning all the ways to get back at Jac. She knew I was coming to the mall. She knew what I wore to school today and that I probably hadn't changed. She must have figured I wouldn't be researching Sean so much after the hallway incident. So she brought my research to me.

"I, um . . . the thing is . . . that wasn't me that called but I think I know—"

"And who is this?" Trent swings his arm around my shoulder, interrupting my confession.

I shrug Trent's arm off. "This is Sean Griswold. He . . . I . . . We go to the same school. Sean, this is my annoying brother, Trent."

Sean holds out his hand and Trent shakes it. "Trent. Right. You almost took state two years ago in swimming, right?"

"Almost." Trent beams. "The punk ahead of me was juicing. You a swimmer?"

"Yeah." Sean scratches his nose. "I'm training for a triathlon right now, but mostly I bike."

Triathlon? Are freshmen allowed to do triathlons? Don't you have to be older and in amazing shape and . . . superhuman to do that?

"Cool," Trent says and means it. "Let me know if you ever want to go swim some laps at the Y or something. I'm buying my boxers, sis, and then we're out. Did you find a bra yet?"

"Shut up," I say. Trent smirks and leaves.

"So," Sean says.

"So," I say.

"That wasn't you that called me, then?"

I shake my head no, afraid that if I open my mouth I'll divulge too much information.

"Weird. I wonder who it was."

"Maybe it could have been another girl in a red shirt."

"Yeah, but hey, I like that shirt."

I get a lot of compliments on this shirt because, in addition to being a color I look good in, it says SERENITY NOW. Most people think it's a tree-hugger thing, like Jac's MAKE LOVE NOT WAR shirt, but it's actually something George's dad says in an episode of *Seinfeld* when he's trying to calm himself down. Most kids my age don't get it; they're too busy watching reality crap, so I feel like I'm walking around wearing my own private joke.

"Thanks."

"Episode 159, right? Final season. One of my favorites. Although I love any episode where George freaks out. Which is pretty much all of them."

He knows the episode number. *He knows the episode number!* Never, in all my fifteen years, have I met someone versed enough in *Seinfeld*ese to know episode numbers! "You . . . you like *Seinfeld*, then?"

Sean shrugs. "More like obsessed. I've got a bunch of memorabilia I bought off eBay and have the whole series on DVD.

I even went one whole day using nothing but catchphrases." He blushes and fingers a folded navy sweater. "Man, when I say it out loud, it all kind of sounds stupid, huh?"

Actually, it is the coolest thing I've ever heard. I mean, he knew the episode number! "No. Well, kind of."

"*Seinfeld*, huh?" Sean squints a little, like he's sizing me up. "I would have guessed your syndicated show of choice would be more like *Friends*."

I roll my eyes. "First off, they hang out at a place called Central Perk. Anything involving the word *perk* nauseates me."

"Understandably so."

"And," I add, building momentum, "the closest thing they have to a Kramer is a Joey. I mean, who would you rather be friends with?"

"Yeah, but Elaine is no Jennifer Aniston."

"Spare me," I say. "The Jerry/Elaine dynamic is far more compelling than that whole Ross/Monica thing."

"I think Monica was Ross's sister."

"Oh. See? I don't even know their names. Not a *Friends* girl."

Sean laughs. "Well, if I ever see a CENTRAL PERK shirt, I know who I'm buying it for."

"Save your money."

Then it's like the conversation is water out of a hose, and someone has turned off the faucet so everything that was flowing so well a second ago is just a slow drip, drip.

"Well," Sean says.

"Yeah," I say.

"I better—"

"Uh-huh."

"Crazy running into you. Let me know if you spot any other red-shirted girls."

I notice he smells good, like peppermint and Ivory soap mixed with tire rubber, but in a good way. Like when you first get a new bike.

While I no doubt smell like that gyro. I look in my bag for some gum and say, "I will. And you let me know if—" I look up and he's already left, leaving me dissecting the conversation and planning how I'm going to grill my meddling BFF.

"Serenity now," I mumble to a nearby faceless mannequin.

NINE

The only thing worse than Jac stalking Sean is Jac stalking me. I ignore her all weekend, skipping the sleepover. But come Monday, she's there after every class, trying to explain, acting like it didn't happen, walking next to me and pointing out how much she's helping me grow.

"Gumdrop," she coos right before third period. She's painted on her Sympathy Look, the one that worked so well on her dad. Back when she used to see him. "You can't be mad at me! I was *helping* you. I did it out of love. Someday you'll thank me."

I grunt, which is the closest thing to a reaction she's gotten. She jumps on it.

"And maybe I went a little too far with the mall thing, but there was just so much potential there. Sean got to see you outside of school. He met your family. Really, my phone call was an act of sheer stalking genius!" She's obviously not sorry and obviously oblivious to her own extreme dementia.

"You're unbalanced," I say.

"So are you. That's why we're friends. We're still friends, right?" She watches me expectantly.

"Yeah. Of course we are." Fighting with Jac is like making a cake from scratch when there's a box of Tastykakes in the pantry. It's not worth the effort.

"Oh, I have some notes for you."

"Notes?" I ask, not liking the sound of the word.

"Well, just ideas, really. I think we need to start in on some drive-bys at this Saturday's sleepover. Figure out what Sean's doing and where he goes after school."

"We don't drive."

"Maybe we can do a walk-by then." Jac runs her tongue along her braces. "Or a run-by. We don't want to look obvious. Maybe a bike-by?"

Before I have time to stop Jac's scheming, the bell rings and Miss Marietta stumbles in front of the class. Her complexion's grimy and her normally stylish hair hangs in a greasy bun. Wild Wednesday on a Sunday night? She slides a DVD into the player and slumps into her seat.

The video's about mating rituals of animals in the Amazon. Miss Marietta must be really hammered to show a video like this to a bunch of teenagers. Then again, it's the first video anyone actually watches with interest. Some students take notes— I doubt for educational purposes.

As fascinating as it is to watch snakes getting hot and heavy, I keep finding myself focusing back on Sean's head. I do a quick log in my journal, hoping the structure of it will help me stay objective.

PFE
February 3
Topic: Five Senses of Sean

1. <u>See</u>: Big—but not too big—head. Blond hair.
   Brownish/goldish eyes. Broad shoulders.
   Skinny waist. Sculpted calves (just calling it
   like I see it).
2. <u>Hear</u>: Regular guy voice. Doesn't use slang/
   swear words like other guys I know. Kind of
   says the word "all" weird, like "ull."
3. <u>Taste</u>: Gross! What am I supposed to do,
   lick him?
4. <u>Smell</u>: Good. Better than most boys. You'd
   think all those years sitting behind him
   I'd notice how he smelled. Now, whenever
   he's in the room, it attacks me like those
   department store perfume ladies who must
   get paid by the spritz.
5. <u>Touch</u>: I don't know if I've ever really
   touched him. Maybe once or twice when
   passing papers back. You know, even
   shorter, his hair looks so soft. Maybe it's
   time I rub it a little. So I can give more
   concrete details.

I stretch my hand across my desk, but stop when I realize
the horror of what I was about to do. Pet Sean. Have I lost my

mind? Why can't I stay on track with this? I picked his head—not his scent, or *Seinfeld* know-how or hair texture.

But something about this guy makes me want to tell him things. To confide in him. To get him to confide in me. Does he feel the same way? Would he still if he knew about this crazy assignment? Maybe I'm like an artist who gets too close to her subject matter. When you do a still-life painting of a bowl of fruit, you don't take a bite of the apple.

Maybe I need to leave Sean, and his head, alone.

♥ ♥ ♥

The cafeteria reeks, which could be because it's Taco Boat day, but more likely it's the sweat of teenagers lined up against the back wall, convulsively fidgeting as they await their report card doom. And for the first report card day in my life, I'm among the nervous throngs.

This used to be my moment. Those letters declaring my educational fate sang. Not that I didn't already know what they were. I would have already added up the percentages myself, checking that the teacher got it right, calculating the exact score I needed on each midterm to achieve an A.

Now I have no clue how I've done on the tests. Ahead of me is a ticking time bomb, one I want to shove into my locker, not take home to my already-don't-know-what-to-do-with-me parents. Except our school is all checks and balances with our grades—giving us a report card in school, sending one to our home, and posting the grades online. They do everything short of spray painting it on the parents' bedroom wall. But maybe I can check the mailbox every day. And give our computer a virus so they can't log on. Maybe I can escape.

Escape is exactly what I want to do when I see Sean three people behind me in the G–L line. Curse that alphabetical connection! He thinks I'm stalking him, and even if this observation isn't entirely off (it's research!), I don't want to give him any more reason to believe it now.

I grab my report card and somehow open the sides without ripping the whole sheet, an amazing feat considering how difficult they make those stupid tear-on-this-line-fold-here-and-don't-rip-here envelopes. I look straight down at the report card to avoid eye contact with Sean, who has retrieved his own and is just within my peripheral vision.

But when I do look at my card, I notice a typo, not in my name where it usually is—people are always replacing the *a* with an *e*—but in the actual grades. There's a B. I can handle that. Who wants to be valedictorian, anyway?

But wait.

C? That's just average. I can't be average. Average is for . . . average people. And yet that is the letter on my report card, right next to the A from the previous quarter. I got a C. In biology.

Breathing is suddenly a very difficult task. I'm rifling through my backpack in pursuit of my brown paper lunch sack and wondering why you breathe in a sack anyway when I hear a voice that is becoming all too familiar.

"How'd you do?" asks Sean.

"Um, all right," I say, breathing more slowly. "Just finding my happy place."

"I thought report card time *is* your happy place. Aren't you the Queen of the Honor Roll?"

I look down and when I look up again, Sean's expression shifts, like he has X-ray vision and can see through my clenched fist, can see the grades, can see through my skull and into my mind that is crunching the numbers in a futile attempt to recalculate the unexpected, can see into my heart and knows that it's beating just a fraction of a hair faster when he looks at me the way he's looking. Like he can see into my soul.

I swallow, fighting the urge to crumple up my report card and stuff it into the trash. But instead, I shove it into Sean's hands and say, "Looks like I've been demoted to Duchess."

Sean whistles. "Marietta killed me too. I think she was drunk when she did grades. No one got an A."

"Really? How do you know what other people got?"

"Well, I don't. Not for sure." Sean blushes. "But it seems like everyone is complaining about their scores and stuff."

"Thanks for trying to make me feel better."

"One C doesn't mean you're not brilliant."

"Just average," I say, even though the use of the word *brilliant* does help soften the blow. "But, did you do all right? Nothing your parents would ground you for?"

"Grounding? My parents don't bother with something like discipline, let alone caring about my grades. But this one is going on the fridge, even if I'm the only one who'll look at it."

"Well, good for you."

"Yeah," he says, his eyes flashing a bit before they crinkle into a smile. "Well, as exciting as discussing my lack of academic direction is, I have to swing over to Coach Jarvis's office and ask him something about swim. See you later, Gritas."

"Later," I say as Sean walks away. But I don't want later, I want now. Now with Sean next to me, so I don't have to face the Grade Goblin alone.

"I like to bike," I blurt out, sounding like I'm reciting from an I-can-read book. See Spot. See Spot Say Stupid Stuff.

Sean cuts back across the cafeteria until he's looking at me face-to-face. "Uh . . . that's great."

"No, I mean . . . maybe we can go on a bike ride sometime?"

"I didn't know you ride."

"I don't. Well, I do. Like around the neighborhood and stuff." I straighten my back. "But I'm looking into getting into like, real bike riding. Maybe."

Sean breaks into a smile. "How I ride . . . it's pretty intense. I don't know if you can handle it."

I smile back, mostly to cover the fear that creeps up my neck. He gets one *Seinfeld* reference and calls me brilliant and suddenly I'm asking to ride with him? So much for scientific objectivity.

"Try me."

TEN

Ms. Callahan's outfit burns my eyes as she greets me outside the office door. Orange skirt with a floral brown top. Pointy burgundy shoes that match her poorly applied lipstick. And hair weeping for some product. I really must save this woman.

"How has your week been?" she asks with a warm smile that exposes lipstick-covered teeth.

"Fine."

"I called you in because I took the liberty of checking your grades. I know you're a bright student. Have you ever gotten a C before?"

"Yes." In second grade. On a spelling pretest.

"Do you want me to talk to any of your teachers? Make them aware of . . . things?"

"No. Just bombed a test. It happens."

"Yes." Ms. Callahan folds her arms across her ample chest. "But does it happen to *you*?"

I stare at the pictures of her obese feline crowding her desk. So she spends all day giving kids too much attention and spends all night giving her cat too much food. "Apparently, it does."

"How are your Focus Exercises going?" she asks, changing course.

I almost smile. "Good. It's . . . fun. I like the . . . order of it. And I'm learning a lot."

"I thought you would. Keep with it." She pauses. "Although, next week I want to try something new."

My stomach lurches. "What's that?"

"The activity is called A Conversation with Dad."

I blink. My mouth opens. Closes. My left leg twitches. "My dad?" I croak.

"Not your actual father."

My leg—my body—relaxes. "Then who?"

"Well, whomever you like. Someone representing your father. It's practice for the time when you're ready to address him face-to-face. So it can be me—"

"Not you." I'm not about to pretend my chubby, Afroed guidance counselor is my bald, cheerful father. "Can I . . . invite a friend?"

"If that's what would make you most comfortable."

"I'll ask my friend Jac. But can I still write about Shha—I mean, my Focus Object?"

Ms. Callahan cocks her head to the side, a peculiar look on her face. "Do you think this Focus Object is really helping you gain introspection?"

"Uh-huh."

"Then, yes, whatever helps. Just make sure you don't focus

too much on this object. There will be a point where you'll need to let go and move on."

Does asking my Focus Object out on a bike riding excursion count as moving on? Didn't think so.

PFE
February 8, afternoon
Topic: Analysis of how I'm focusing on . . . focusing.

→ I think I've figured out a way to maintain emotional distance from my Focus Object, yet still further my research.
→ I will still write about Sean's head, but now I'm going to get INSIDE it.
→ I've set the goal of asking him five questions on our bike ride.
→ It's arbitrary, but it feels like the next logical step (if any of this can be considered logical).

It's warm out for a Pennsylvania winter. So warm, I slip off my sweater and go outside in nothing but a long-sleeved shirt and jeans. Dirty patches of snow melt into the yellow grass. The air smells overly sweet, like a car air freshener that's just been unwrapped. I kick a rock across the cracked driveway, watching it bounce until it hits the garage door. The sunlight glints on the basketball hoop.

It's been almost two months—an eternity—since I last played. Basketball used to be scheduled in right between homework and my self-allotted hour of TV. It isn't in my schedule anymore. I don't *have* a schedule anymore.

I grab a basketball out of the garage and bounce it once or twice against the concrete. The smell of the rubber envelops me like teammates in a time-out huddle. I close my eyes and shoot the ball into a perfect arch. I don't have to open them to know the ball has gone in. The chains cheer.

A few more shots can't hurt. Dad and I used to shoot every Thursday, until he got MS. Then our shooting became more sporadic, based on how he was feeling, I suppose, not that I knew that at the time. I think of the failed baskets I witnessed from my window that day. Even though his playing isn't always that weak, Dad is never going to fully get his game back. One more relapse, and he may lose his shot completely. Although, seriously, that's the least of his worries.

Now I'm pumping the ball harder, maneuvering around invisible opponents. The crowd in my head roars louder with each fake out, each shot. I'm about to win the one-person championship when someone coughs. The applause ends. I drop the ball. My dad is standing on the walkway, his famous grin overtaking his face.

"Don't stop now, sunshine. I think you're about to win the game."

"Oh. Hi."

His smile doesn't fade. He's so elated with his discovery, at my momentary athletic relapse, that his face is close to exploding. His hope is too much for me. "Can I shoot a few with you?" he asks.

I fix him with a stare cold enough to melt the warmth of his smile. I want to freeze him there, so he can't move. So he can't feel. "No. You can't."

"Why not?" He shrugs. "Think I'll take you?"

No, I mean—you can't. This isn't wheelchair basketball. I laugh at my own cruelty. It worries me, this monster inside. The monster who would hurt someone already feeling so much pain. I choke on my laugh, trying to stop the familiar rise of emotion from surfacing. The truth, I know, is that it's not my dad I'm really mad at. I'm mad at his disease.

And it's not anger. It's fear.

"Sorry. Gotta go," I say, brushing past him and into the house. Into the bathroom, to wash the smell of rediscovery off my hands. To wash the tears of self-loathing off my face.

ELEVEN

Bike ride with Sean is today. My bike still has neon spokes and I haven't been on it in a year. Not to worry. After all, riding a bike is like . . . riding a bike. You get on and go. A much bigger problem is clothes. I know hard-core cyclists wear tight clothes, but I don't do spandex. The devil wears spandex. And I doubt the devil's butt is as big as mine. Jac even had me try on a bunch of potential biking outfits—nothing worked. (But it's hard not to love her. She's the cheer mom who memorizes all her daughter's routines and does them in the bleachers during a game.)

After further deliberation, I throw a pair of basketball shorts over Jac's fuchsia yoga capri pants and ride my bike out of the cul-de-sac and onto the trail that will lead me into Valley Forge National Park. The weather is warmer than yesterday, but the clouds promise a change soon. I switch the gears of my Schwinn before heading up a small incline. This is exercise, not a sport. Bike riding isn't competitive. And my dad doesn't have a bike. This activity feels safe, although I don't get the same rush I did yesterday with the ball.

Even with the extra padding, my butt is already complaining about the seat. By the time I cover the four miles to the park, I'm ready to take a break. But there's Sean, stretching his legs next to the Visitors' Center entrance. He has on the expected biker shorts, with a blue jacket, helmet, gloves, and those weird shoes I saw when I began my stalking/research adventures. I feel self-conscious about my outfit and about the star stickers I stuck on my helmet in seventh grade.

"Hey," I say and plop down next to him. "Sorry I'm late. I had to bike over from my house."

"Where do you live?"

"Near Audubon. You?"

"Collegeville."

"Collegeville?" I gasp. "But that's like ten miles away."

"Usually I bike down to the city."

"You mean Philadelphia?"

"No, New York."

I gasp again. He laughs.

"I'm joking, Payton. Yes, Philadelphia. But I thought I'd take it easy on you today and just do the loop."

"Okay. Not that I need any special treatment. I know how to ride a bike, you know."

Sean smiles. "Have you ever done this loop before?"

I stand up and throw my leg over the bike. I don't like Sean looking at me like that. Like I'm a scrub. I've played sports my whole life. I can do this. Easy. "Yeah, all the time. I'm surprised we haven't seen each other here."

Sean rubs his chin, his eyes dancing. "I'll draft then. Let's stop at the arch monument, then Washington's Headquarters. We'll skip the hill—"

"I can do the hill," I insist. I did a hill getting here. How bad can it be?

"We'll see. Just stay with me." Sean clicks his shoes into the pedals of his bike and readjusts his helmet. He takes a sip from his water bottle and spits it out. I do the same, except I choke on the water and end up coughing. Sean just shakes his head and starts to ride.

We pass by the bunkers that Revolutionary War soldiers slept in back before heating and Serta mattresses were around. Valley Forge has a different feel than say, Gettysburg, because there weren't actual battles here. This was the rebels' camp for six months and they endured all sorts of terrors like hunger, disease, and lack of outdoor plumbing. But this place puts things into perspective for me. I'm thinking about how much my butt hurts when I remember they had to walk through the snow with bloody feet. I'm worried that I won't make it through a bike ride while the soldiers didn't know if they'd live through the next day.

We weave around the dog-walkers and tourists along the path. My bike is the equivalent of a Ford Escort and Sean's riding a Beamer. I see him tightening the resistance on his bike while waiting for me to catch up. A smile is set on my face so Sean doesn't know how hard I'm working.

We make it to the arch, and Sean stops to take a drink. He's obviously doing this for me because he hasn't broken a sweat and isn't even close to winded. I, however, guzzle half my water bottle.

Time to start in on my questions. Not that I have any prepared. I figure I'll just see where the moment takes us.

Sean unzips his jacket pocket and unveils a bottle of Advil.
He pops it open and knocks back three pills.

"Are you an addict?" I blurt out.

Sean seems to contemplate this for a minute. "That'd be a
pretty lame addiction. Advil. I mean, if I was going to be a user,
I'd be a little more extreme, you know? Don't want the other
druggies making fun."

"You didn't answer my question."

Sean shrugs. "I get headaches. Lately I've been getting
them more and more. Pretty soon I'm going to have to give
up the ibuprofen and move to the hard stuff."

"Like?"

"Excedrin." Sean swigs some more water.

Headaches. I can relate to headaches. First question down.
Now . . . "You ever come riding with your brother?"

"That would be hard, being as I'm an only child."

"Oh. So who lives with—" I freeze. Sean doesn't know Jac
and I called him the other day. Sean doesn't know any of our
investigative . . . techniques. "I mean, so how often do you ride?"

Sean leans against his handlebars. "Almost every day when
the weather is good. Longer rides on weekends. I focus more on
swimming and running in winter, and take a few spin classes at
the Y when the snow keeps me off the road."

"Didn't you tell my brother you're doing a triathlon?"

"Yeah. This summer. It's a sprint—there aren't many bigger
ones with divisions for my age. In a few years I'll work up to

some of the national competitions. My main goal is to win the Ironman someday."

Which leads to Question #4: "What makes you want to do that?"

"It's the biggest high. And the test of the ultimate athlete. I want to be the strongest. I want to be the best."

"Yeah, but *why*?"

"I don't know." Sean gives me a sideways glance. "It's complicated. Why do you like basketball?"

I rub at a scuff on my shoes. I'm supposed to be asking the questions here. "I quit basketball."

"Really?" Sean looks surprised. "That was always your sport in junior high."

The tiniest thrill runs up my spine. He remembered I played basketball. Granted, before I quit the team, I wore the jersey to school on game days. But, still—he remembered. "I gave it up a month or two ago."

"So you don't like it anymore?"

"I didn't say that."

"Then why'd you quit?"

I tilt my head to the side. "It's complicated."

"Touché." Sean's expression grows thoughtful. "But it can't be that complicated. If it's not your thing, that's fine. But if you love something, you hold on to it."

"You always this deep when you ride?" I ask.

Sean laughs. "Nah, usually I just try to hit squirrels that get in my way. Let's see if we can run some over." He clicks his shoes into his pedals and takes off.

He's joking. Totally. But just to make sure, I whistle every now and then to warn any unsuspecting rodents.

Everything around us is dead—the trees, the grass, the sky. It's like we're stuck in a black-and-white movie with no color, just varying degrees of gray. Even the sunlight, seeping through the clouds, has a dingy hue. We ride past the arch, downhill to an open field with deer galore. Sean veers off the road toward a crop of trees sloping upward. I shift gears and follow.

The hill is murder. Without Sean around, I'd jump off and walk my bike up. I'm standing on the pedals now, pumping my legs and leaning forward. The hill doesn't let up, getting steeper and steeper with each turn of my wheels. We've probably only done a half of a mile, but it feels like I'm scaling Everest. It's the most intense thing I've ever done. Sean's ahead of me, but not far and he keeps looking back to make sure I'm with him.

"You good?" he calls.

"Yeah."

But I'm not.

My head is spinning. I can't get my legs to pedal anymore. It's like my body has an instant power outage. I stumble off my bike and kneel on the gravel, managing to get my helmet off before I throw up what seems like gallons of water. When I'm done, I contemplate lying down in the middle of the road to let a car finish me off. I'm already half-dead.

Sean is beside me now, forcing me to drink some water before he pours more onto my face and hair. He zips off his jacket and balls it up into a pillow, which I gratefully lie on. Next, he lifts my legs and massages my calves.

Horror—I didn't shave my legs today. Did I yesterday? It's winter! I should be safe from male contact. I spend my whole adolescence shaving compulsively and one of the few times I forget is when the action happens. But this isn't action. Is it?

He doesn't seem to notice the prickly hair; his attention is on the knotted muscles. Up and down his hands slide. Heat rises in my face and it's not from biking. This is the closest I've been with a boy, but the vomited water next to me nixes any romantic ideas.

"Whew. I'm sorry." He raises his arm and wipes his brow. "I shouldn't have taken us up the hill. Next time I'll let you borrow one of my bikes, okay? And we'll skip the hill."

"Next time?" I close my eyes.

"You have to do it, and soon, or else you'll never touch a bike again. I threw up the first time I rode this hill too. Right after I crashed."

My eyes flutter open and I look up at Sean. Time for the final question. "Is that how you got that scar on your forehead? You crashed your bike?"

His hands pause midmassage. "No. Not from a crash. Something else."

I'm about to ask him more, when a pair of bikers call ahead for us to move. I scramble up and lug my bike farther off the trail.

"You ready to finish?" Sean asks.

I choke on my words. "You want . . . Are you serious?"

"Nah. We can walk back." Sean chuckles. "You know, I never knew you were this fun to tease."

"There's a lot you don't know about me," I say as I pick up my helmet and loop it onto my handles.

Sean's voice softens. "I don't doubt it." And then even softer, soft enough I almost don't hear, he says, "But I wouldn't mind changing that."

We're silent as we walk down the hill. As if to punctuate the change in mood, the clouds open up and it begins to rain. I'm freezing. I can still taste vomit. My legs are on fire.

And I can't remember the last time I felt this good.

PFE
Feb 9
Topic: Cold Hard Facts learned based upon five questions experiment.

1. Sean is an only child. So we do not know who answered the phone when Jac called.
2. He pops pills because he gets headaches.
3. He wants to be the next Ironman.
4. He likes to feel in control.
5. I still don't know where the scar came from. Although, I wasn't focusing on it much once his jacket came off.* Hello, arm muscles.

*Sorry, I'm dehydrated and the searing pain in my buns is causing me to not think straight. I *shouldn't objectify Sean like that (although he is a Focus Object so maybe . . .).*

Sorry again. Fatigue-driven delirium is setting in.

♥ ♥ ♥

"Tell me about it again," Jac insists, popping a third cheesecake bite into her mouth. It's our Saturday sleepover, I've already told her about the ride twice, and I'm wondering how much longer she'll keep talking before I pass out from exhaustion.

"There's nothing to tell. We went on a bike ride. We had fun. I want to surgically remove my butt. Nothing big."

"Did he say anything flirty?"

"No, we were bike riding. And it wasn't like a stroll along the beach. It was extreme."

"I want to go on a bike ride." She balls up her cheesecake wrapper and pantomimes steering a bike over to the trash. "I bet he'll take us. Let's call him and ask."

"I don't think—"

"You don't think what? Why can't I go too?"

"It's just—"

Jac points at me. "Aha! You like him, don't you?"

"Well . . ."

"You do! You do! Admit it."

My heart flutters for a moment but my head stays clear. "No. I don't like him. Not like that."

"But you care if I call him. You've never cared what boys I bring along with us before."

"That's because they're random. I never know them. So they're all the same to me."

"So even better if we hang out with a guy you *do* know. Plus, you're getting your homework done at the same time. It's like a Payton dream come true." Jac flicks on the TV, like it's not a big deal. Like she really is going to take this to another level.

It's a Very Big Deal. Something changed today between me and Sean and I don't want to mess it up by being too aggressive. If I give Jac any inkling about the weirdness I felt when he massaged my legs, she could go *matchmaker* on me. Last time she tried that, I ended up behind the swings with Anthony Barbarini, trying to convince him not to shove his tongue down my throat, and my only method of persuasion was a harsh kick in the groin. I don't want my relationship with Sean to end as abruptly.

"Jac. Can you drop this?"

She turns down the TV and looks at me. "If you want me to, sure. But why quit now? You could have a good time with him, if you let yourself. And I think you could really use that."

Oh . . . fine. I give up. "Okay. We can all go on a ride together. Maybe he can even bring more boys."

Jac squeals. "Huzzah! The more boys, the more joys. Especially if they're all in spandex."

"Speaking of spandex," I say, grabbing Jac's hand so she stops her channel surfing. "Look at what that woman is wearing."

We groan together. Lifetime movie. The perfect subject changer.

"I wish I could go back in time to the eighties and offer

fashion help to that sad woman," Jac says. "She's famous and she still wasn't saved from the bangs of death."

"I've seen this one!" Like I should actually be proud I've wasted two hours of my life on an old Lifetime network movie. "The mom gets breast cancer, and gets the lump removed and decides to get fake boobs and starts dating younger men . . ."

Jac squints at the TV. "Maybe my mom can try out if they do a remake. Change it."

"No! It's sad. I can't remember how it ends, but I remember it's sad."

We watch as Spandex Woman waves as her teenage daughter leaves on a date, then slips into the hall closet and starts sobbing hysterically. The next scene is of the mom in a hospital bed. No spandex now. Bangs still surprisingly high, though.

"Mom," says the daughter. "I thought you'd fought this. The doctors said the chances of this happening again were so small—why didn't you tell us you were sick again?"

"I wanted you to enjoy your prom . . . I wanted . . ." Tears. Hugs. Hazy close-up. "Doctors don't know everything. But I don't regret the surgery, even if it might have masked the remaining tumor. You see, my breasts finally made me feel like a woman. Well, those men made me feel like a wom—"

"Oh, please. Turn it off."

"Wait," I said.

"Mom, it's only prom. I just wish you would have told me. I wish I knew this could happen. I thought the worst was over, and now—"

Tears slip down my face. The mom's hospital monitor flat-lines and a bunch of nurses rush in, pushing the daughter out of

94

the way. "Mom! This isn't supposed to happen! You weren't supposed to die! They were just boobs!"

Jac finally stands up and turns off the TV. "Tell me you aren't crying."

I wipe my eyes with my sleeve. "I'm not."

"Because it's different, you know. For you. I don't know what it's like . . . My dad wouldn't have even cared enough to lie. You're lucky, in a way."

"I said I wasn't crying. It's just a movie."

Jac shrugs and leaves to get ready for bed. I nestle under the covers and decide the bike ride aftermath has made me hallucinate. For some reason, in the last shot of the movie, I could have sworn Spandex Woman looked like my dad.

"Hey." Jac pokes her head out from the bathroom, mouth full of toothpaste. "I forgot. Sean. Hot. Spandex?"

"I'm going to sleep now."

"Muscles. Bigger." Jac stops to spit. "Did you see that?"

I imagine Sean without his shirt, and face the wall so she doesn't see me blush. "Good night, Jac."

"Someday you're going to notice, honeybuns." Jac turns off the light and slips into bed. "Maybe not with Sean, but someday you won't think I'm so off."

I don't think Jac is off at all, and that idea is what keeps me up for most of the night.

95

TWELVE

"Have you gotten your report card yet?" Mom asks.

"No," I lie. "Next week."

Brochures and a huge atlas are spread across a table at Pisano's, my family's favorite guaranteed-to-give-you-heartburn pizza place. I tap my feet in rhythm with Elvis singing "Don't Be Cruel" but stop because it's too much effort to unstick them with each upbeat. Germs everywhere. I attack my hands with sanitizer, rubbing the liquid into each fingertip. I don't look up at my mom.

"Next week?" Mom looks confused. "I could have sworn—"

"Next week," I say, this time more firmly.

"Oh. I'm sure you told me. Not that we don't already know you've done well." She smiles. "I just want to get a copy for your scrapbook."

Your copy is already in the trash. Sorry I didn't preserve the memory. I'm sure my first C is a moment to cherish.

Trent's on his cell and Dad is staring into space, frowning. He's in a rare sour mood. Usually, he'll pretend to feel fine but he's not bothering today. A report card revelation would not help.

Trent clicks off his phone and clears his throat. "I'd like to call this meeting to order. Operation Plan Spring Break has begun. First item of business?"

How about changing the name to Dad's Going to Relapse, You Idiots. Not that I share my clever name for the outing. It's too many syllables.

This is a first for our family, planning a vacation beyond a car ride down to DC. Actually, it's our first trip since Caleb left for school and we abandoned family outings so the boys could enjoy a brotherly bonding trip somewhere with lots of sun and girls. My brothers plan their trips all year, and yet they're giving it up. Which leads me to wonder—is this a vacation, or a farewell?

"I think first"—Mom pushes a plate of buffalo wings aside so we can get a better view of the map of the Caribbean—"we need to figure out where everyone wants to go."

"Hawaii," says Trent.

"Key Largo," says Dad.

"And I'm thinking Belize," Mom says, riffling through her brochures. "What about you, Payton?"

"Alaska."

Everyone stares at me.

"Alaska?" Dad shakes his head. "Why would we go there?"

"It's cold."

"The point is to warm up over spring break," Trent says. "Maybe meet some girls and really heat things up."

Dad rolls his eyes. "Creative idea for a family trip."

"Well, I haven't researched Alaska." Mom frowns. "I don't think anyone else would be interested in going there. No offense. Caleb gets enough gloomy weather in London and personally, I want to go somewhere I can tan."

"Think about it," I say, exceeding my usual allotment of syllables. "This trip is a suicide mission."

"Payton! Don't say that," Mom says.

Trent snorts, trying to make a joke of it. "How is it a suicide mission? What, you going to go cliff jumping and miss the water?"

The waitress brings our pizza and I devote my attention to inhaling mine. The booth hurts my butt, although any kind of sitting stings. My family goes through each brochure, discussing the pros and cons of the various resorts. Finally, my dad nudges me. "Can you try to act excited? Check out this place in Florida. We can go see the Miami Heat play. Maybe find an old Shaq bobblehead. Maybe even see something scandalous like the team skinny dipping."

"I'm down if they're with some desperate fans!" Trent adds.

I shrug him off. *Listen to yourself, Dad. The team name is Heat. Meaning they are located in a place where there is HEAT! Remember Cancun—the place where your MS symptoms started? Now you're thinking about going on another trip? Do you want to end up in a wheelchair?*

"It's too hot" is all I say.

"You're being stubborn, Payton," Dad says. "What's going on? Are you worried about my MS?"

"Someone needs to be."

Dad runs a hand down his face. "We've thought this out

98

already. Got the okay from my doctor. Heat can cause a flare-up, but so can any number of things."

This is the most I've talked to my parents about any of this. A tiny bead of sweat trails down my back. "But you're still going to risk it."

"It's not about risk." His voice has a slight edge to it. "I don't understand why you're acting like this. It's a trip."

"You don't need to get mad at me."

"I'm not . . . I'm not mad." Dad lets out a breath and shakes his head. "Look, I don't know how long I'll be able to do things like this with you. I want to take advantage of it while I can."

"Yeah, you brat," Trent says. "Be glad your dad even wants to do something with you."

Their anger feels good, much better than worry. I grab a slice of pizza and stand up. "You all know how I feel, not that it matters. I'll wait outside."

I rush out of the restaurant. It's raining again, so I sit under an awning and finish my soggy pizza. My family joins me twenty minutes later and no one says a word the entire way home.

♥ ♥ ♥

After another tense weekend, I'm ready to get to school and enjoy the carefree lifestyle of a fifteen-year-old. You know, hanging with friends. Eating a nice lunch. Which is what I'm about to do, until Jac plops her lunch tray down by Sean.

We aren't even on our side of the cafeteria! I swear, the whole universe groaned at our blatant rebellion of the high school caste system. Sean sits at the I'm-too-into-sports-to-care-about-girls-yet table. So if you're a girl, you don't go there. Unless you're the butch goalie on the hockey team, and even she sits at the edge of the group.

But Jac is oblivious to the ways of the world, or acts like she is. She just flicks her braids and turns to Sean. "So when are we going on a bike ride?"

We? WE! Since when does she become a WE with Sean?

Sean smiles, but when he speaks, he looks at me. "It's a full moon tonight. Supposed to be clear skies. We could do a late-night ride."

Even with appropriate bike gear, riding at night is not always safe. Plus, there might be lunatics, *real* lunatics, waiting to jump out of the trees and abduct us. "Jac's got theater stuff and I—"

"Sounds exciting." Jac grins at Sean. At least the other boys at the table give her the same look of disgust. "Maybe you can bring some friends too. Do you have any friends who like to bike?"

Sean bites into his sandwich. "Sure. I'll bring them along. Maybe a quarter or so after nine. Sound good to you, Payton?"

"I don't know—"

"He'll go easy on you this time, right, Sean? You sure worked her the other day. She's been talking about it all week-end. All weekend."

Sean swallows and coughs. "Really? Didn't you like it? If we go tonight, I'll set an easier course."

Blood pumps into my face like air into a tire. Shut up, Jac. "The last course was *fine*. I rode it, didn't I? Jac's the one I'd be worried about. Shopping is her idea of exercise."

Jac laughs. "We'll see you tonight then. And bring those friends in case we need someone to carry us home."

The bell rings and I wait until Sean is gone to pull Jac to the side. "What was that?"

"What? The bike ride? You said it was fine."

"Not that. Your cantankerous attitude."

"Can't-what-a-cus?"

"Rude. You were being rude."

Jac's eyes are all innocence. "I was *teasing* you, schnookums. That's what you do around boys. I wasn't trying to be mean. And I thought it was cute when Sean looked all concerned about you."

Yeah, he did. But why is she the one pointing that out? I'm confused enough about my feelings right now, not just with Sean, but with life. I don't like feeling rushed into stuff like this. I rub my left shoulder. Maybe a well-designed Focus Exercise would calm me down.

When I don't say anything, Jac sighs. "Look, I'm sorry. I was just doing what we talked about on Saturday. The wild and crazy have-some-fun plan I came up with, remember?"

I roll my eyes.

"And you know this will be awesome. I'll meet you at the corner by your house at nine. Mom is out of town and my sister won't care."

"My parents would never go for it."

"Hello? Then don't *tell* them. Aren't you supposed to be going through a rebellious phase right now?"

I'm torn. If I don't go, Jac will. And she might cause more damage. Plus, I did have fun with Sean the other day. An easier ride might give us more of a chance to talk. But my parents would rage if I snuck out. It's one thing to not talk to them, it's another to use their inability to disclose a family crisis as an excuse to practice inappropriate adolescent behavior.

I shake my head. Wow. That reasoning sounded *way* too much like Ms. Callahan for me to listen to it. Jac's right. I've never snuck out, never lied to my parents, never jumped off a cliff. What is holding me back? Maybe the best way to learn more about myself is to stop being . . . myself.

Besides, if I get caught, what are they really going to do? Send me to a counselor? Ground me from spring break?

"Fine. We'll go. And it might even be fun. But you better wear protective headgear."

Jac throws back her head and laughs. She's still laughing when she leaves me at my locker.

I don't know what's so funny. Bike safety is no laughing matter.

THIRTEEN

I'm delicate with my parents at dinner. After Sunday, they are worried, and worried equals more attentive. I don't want them deciding we need a late-night chat and then discovering I've disappeared. So I talk a little, smile a little, and claim my monthly visitor is not being friendly. This makes Mom sympathetic, Dad uneasy, and Trent completely disgusted. It's enough that they leave me alone for the night.

As part of the show, I walk down my hallway to say good night a little before nine. I contemplate holding a warm water bottle against my side, but sometimes less is more. Although I might want to pack one for the ride—my butt is already shuddering at the inevitable.

I knock softly on my parents' door but no one responds. Cracking the door a bit, I peer inside.

Dad's sitting on the edge of the bed buttoning up his flannel pajama top. Correction—*trying* to button his flannel pajama top. His fingers aren't cooperating and his lips press together in frustration. It's like watching a four-year-old tie his shoelaces.

"Need help?" Mom asks as she appears from the bathroom. She's wearing one of her long, satin nightgowns, the kind I used to sneak into her closet to rub against my cheek.

Dad smiles. "I've performed oral reconstructive surgery. I think I can button a shirt."

Mom watches him for another moment before whispering, "Is it getting bad again, Wayne?"

"Just tired." Dad finishes the last button and kisses my mom on the cheek. "Nothing to worry about."

Mom nods, but her look proves she doesn't believe him and neither do I. I push the door open and try my best to pretend I didn't witness the scene. "Just wanted to say good night."

"Feeling better, sunshine?"

I should be asking him this. Even while dealing with his own pain, he thinks about someone else. Why can't he be mean? Why can't he have a woeful, self-involved, I'm-sick-screw-it phase where he eats Chinese food while watching game shows all day?

"Feeling great. Well, night." I'm about to close the door behind me but poke my head through the crack.

"Oh, and about spring break."

Mom and Dad exchange a loaded look.

"Florida's not bad."

I shut the door quickly and plod to my room. I slip Dad's Sixers shirt onto my pillow like a pillowcase and clutch it, pretending that I'm hugging my dad, like I can squeeze all his pain away.

I'm glad I didn't stay to see their reaction to my Florida

comment. Mom's probably gaping or even worse, tearing up. That I can handle. But what I don't want to see is the look of hope that would be in my dad's eyes. Because it'll ache that much more when I hurt him again.

♥ ♥ ♥

"Who are you trying to be? Catwoman?" I ask Jac when I bike up to the corner of Pawlings Road. She's in black gloves and head-to-toe black spandex, with her hair freed from its braids and flowing under her helmet.

"Meow."

"You're going to freeze. It's forty-something degrees out."

"This spandex is fully lined."

I pull out the extra sweatshirt I've stuffed into my backpack along with some water, hand warmers, and safety flares. Just in case. "Take this."

She grabs the sweatshirt but ties it around her waist.

"And you're supposed to wear bright colors when night riding," I say.

"Duh." She whisks some glow-in-the-dark necklaces out of her pocket and starts fastening them around various parts of her body. "Doesn't mean I can't do it in style."

"Let's go," I say before I decide she is too much of a hazard and call the whole thing off.

The park we're meeting Sean at is only a few blocks away, and we're there in less than five minutes. The park closes at dusk and, luckily, there isn't a ranger in sight. For a moment, I think we've been stood up. Then a maroon Honda Civic with three bikes on a rack swerves into the parking lot and parks in a spot behind the restrooms.

"Is that them?" I ask Jac.

"Let's find out."

"But what if it isn't—" I start to say. She's already covered half the lot.

It could be a car full of criminals looking for high school girls to feed on. Or some weird extremists who kidnap young girls for their cult. Or undercover cops, here to arrest the delinquent youth loitering at the park after hours.

Oh. Or it could be Sean. He gets out of the backseat and waves while the driver slams his door shut. Whoever is in the passenger seat stays there, and even when I get closer I can't see who it is.

"Hey girls," Sean says. "This is my cousin, Mark. He and I ride together all the time. Mark, this is Payton and this is Jac."

Mark nods. "What's up?"

Even in the dark, I can see the familiar look in Jac's eyes. There is no denying it, Mark is hot. He has Sean's same hair and easy smile, but he's older and more chiseled looking. Catwoman is ready to pounce.

"Do you live around here?" Jac asks him.

"Yeah. Just up in Limerick. You?"

Jac flips her hair. "No. I live in Audubon with my mom"—she lowers her voice—"who is never around."

Mark grins. "Lack of parental units. I can dig on that."

The kid in the passenger seat opens his door and spits.

"Grady, get out," Sean says. "I need your help pulling the bikes down."

I still can't see what Grady looks like but I can hear him as he lets out a string of swear words before yanking the bikes off the rack. Finally, he looks up at Jac and me and scowls. She doesn't flinch but I start to shake. I am facing a fate worse than prowling criminals. I'm about to go biking with Vampire Boy.

He's dressed head to toe, as usual, in black. He snorts at Jac and says, "What's with the Day-Glo crap? We riding bikes or going to a rave?"

Sean is already on the ground, putting on his shoes and helmet. "Ignore him. Full moons make him grumpy."

So he's not a vampire but a werewolf. Lovely.

"It's my version of bike safety," Jac says. "People can see me."

Grady walks over and snaps off one of her necklaces. "We're riding in a state park after hours. If anyone sees you, we'll get kicked out. Save your fashion statement for the Fourth of July, would ya?"

Jac's mouth hangs open but she removes the remaining jewelry. Grady turns his attention to me and scrutinizes my bright yellow North Face jacket.

"And what do we have here?"

"I can't take off my jacket," I protest. "I'll freeze."

"You're not taking off your jacket." Sean stands up and clicks his shoes into his pedals. "And Jac, you can wear the jewelry if you want. I've ridden here a million times at night and never gotten caught. No one cares."

Grady shrugs and leans on his bike. "Fine. But if these little divas slow us down—"

Sean laughs. "Grady, you've been slowing me down since fourth grade."

"And what kind of guy complains about having hot girls alone with him at night?" Mark adds.

Jac's twinkling glance asks Did you hear him just call us hot? A chilly breeze rustles the trees and I point to the sweatshirt around her waist. She shakes her head and sticks out her chest.

"You guys can ride and we'll follow," Jac says.

Mark offers her his smooth grin. "And miss the view? I'll stay behind you."

Gagfest. Finally, FINALLY, Sean starts down the path and we trail behind. Even though the sky is clear and the moon is bright, it's still hard to see through some of the denser patches. The naked trees cast shadows across the yawning river, which joins the shore so abruptly, it'd be easy to ride right in. Thinner dirt trails snake off the main cement road, leading into thicker forest. Our circling bike pedals provide a rhythmic hum but don't completely drown out the occasional twig snapped by whatever animals are hiding in the darkness.

I bike as close as I can to Sean and as far from Grady as possible. At least I don't feel his stare on me and he seems content to ride far behind the rest of us. Sean points out little novelties, like the log over the river and the raccoon in the trash can as Mark and Jac flirt behind us.

Jac: I know I've seen you before!

Mark: Nah, I'd remember someone as cute as you.

Jac: But that's how *I* remember *you.*

We hit an incline and stop talking to concentrate. We're almost to the top when I hear a grunt. I turn around to see Grady face down in the dirt, his bike to his side with the wheel spinning just above his head.

He lifts his head and brushes the dirt and leaves out of his face. "Suck. My bike hit a pothole or something."

Sean and Mark are already off their bikes and on the ground, laughing. I cover my mouth to hide my own smile.

"Shut up," Grady says. "I think I hurt my ankle."

Sean is beside him in an instant, inspecting his leg. "You idiot. It's twisted. How'd you manage that?"

"Are you going to help me or criticize me?"

Sean looks up at Mark. "Why don't you walk him down to the car? We'll stay here with the bikes. You can drop him off at home and come back for the rest of us."

"Rest of us?" Jac asks. "I'm going with Mark!"

Sean raises an eyebrow. "Why's that?"

She takes off her helmet, unleashing her hair in all its golden glory. "He'll need help walking Grady down. And I don't want to sit out here at night. Creeps me out."

"I can walk down by myself!" Grady tries to stand up on the ankle but grimaces.

"Stop trying to be the martyr," says Mark. "It's like a mile to the car. Jac and I will carry you down, get you a Band-Aid, fluff your pillow—"

Grady looks like he is going to bite Mark, but he loops his arm over Mark's shoulder anyway. He barely touches Jac's arm and she doesn't push it. She turns and winks at me. "You two be good," she says.

They ease Grady down the hill and disappear around a corner. The only sound is the chirp of an insomniac bird.

And just like that, we're alone.

FOURTEEN

"Told you this ride would be easier than the last one." Sean shakes his head and sits down on a log next to the trail and massages his temples. "Good thing too. Grady was starting to give me another headache."

He's so casual about the whole episode I can't stand it. And I'm still a little in shock about the vampire encounter. "Why are you hanging out with Grady?" I ask.

"What, he didn't win you over with his friendly personality?"

"He's a goth."

"Really? I thought he was more emo. With a punk edge. Old-school punk though, not like Hot Topic style—"

"He has fangs."

"Sure. Goth it is." Sean shrugs. "But so what? Labels are stupid. Do you like it when people call you an uptight prep?"

My mouth hangs open. "No one calls me that!"

"Not to your face. And Grady's the goth, I guess. I'm not sure what I am. Borderline nerd maybe? Wannabe jock? What do you think?"

"I think . . . I think . . . Don't change the subject! Even if you took away Grady's freakishness, he's still a jerk. Why is someone like *you* hanging out with someone like *him*?"

"It's a long story."

I look up the trail where the injured and company have disappeared. "We've got time."

Sean pats the space on the log next to him and I sit. We're close, but not too close. Nothing is touching. Not yet. "See this scar?" he says, pointing to the mystery that is the base of my Sean Stalking. "This is how I met Grady."

"Did he knife you?" I ask, aghast.

Sean laughs. "Hardly. It was the summer before fourth grade and I was at the community pool, trying to swim the full length—no breathing—for the first time. Well, I . . . kind of passed out in the water and hit my head on the side of the pool. Pathetic, I know.

"The pool was packed and the lifeguard didn't see me. But Grady did. He jumped in, dragged me out, and even got the cute lifeguard to do CPR on me."

"So now you're indebted to him," I say.

He shook his head. "I paid him back. See, Grady was there with some other foster kids from the state. I convinced my mom to take him in. But the thing with my mom is she starts all these projects and never finishes them. Like she'll volunteer to do a charity luncheon but she's not going to stick around to clean up. So once she realized that a foster kid requires . . . effort, she flaked out." Sean flicks a bug off the log. "Grady got sucked back into the system until his dad got out of jail last year. Now he lives with him, but spends a lot of time at our house still. I think he wears all black so you can't tell he only has three shirts. He's . . . There's more to him than he puts out there."

"If you say so."

"Really. You'll see."

Right. Like I have any plans of hanging out with Vampire Boy ever again. Schedule it in right after my lunch date with Lord Voldemort. "And what is that scar now? Some symbol of your friendship?"

"Honestly?" Sean looks down. "The day I almost drowned was the day I decided I wanted to do triathlons. I remember feeling so . . . weak and powerless in the water. A total scrub. I never wanted that again."

"Oh," I say, because I'm lousy at thoughtful remarks. The scar story explains a lot about Sean, but it's still a bit of a disappointment. Some of Jac's wild ideas had managed to rub off on me, and even though a near drowning is newsworthy, I'd been hoping for a knifing.

"Doesn't Grady ever get to you, though? The whole I-am-death thing?"

"But that's what I'm trying to tell you. That's not him at all, just how you perceive him. It's like, you could go dress yourself in a potato sack, and you'd still look . . ."

Say good. Or if I'm being greedy, beautiful. But good will do.

". . . like you. It doesn't change who you are. Haven't you ever looked past your first impression and seen more?"

Exhibit A was sitting right in front of me. My initial impression of Sean, the impression that'd stuck for almost seven years, was that he was blocking the board. That's it. No thoughts about his likes or dislikes. Who he was. He was the boy with the head.

How many people do I know like that—the school counselor with the Afro, the teacher with a hangover, or the goth kid with the fangs. Yet, through Sean I was seeing them as different people with their own stories.

Sean rests his chin on his knees before picking up a stick and drawing a circle in the dirt. "Okay, so your turn."

"My turn? What do you mean?"

Sean turns his head to the side and smiles. The corners of his eyes crinkle, like my dad's but in a very I-don't-think-of-you-like-my-dad sort of way. A chill runs down my neck. "Oh, c'mon. You're always asking me questions. And I don't know anything about you. Where's the dirt?"

"There is no dirt. I'm totally clean. Boring. Sorry."

"It's the boring people who have something to hide. Tell me why you quit basketball."

I lick my lips. Suddenly my mouth is dry. "I just wasn't into it anymore."

"Why not?"

"I don't know. I can't explain it. Something changed and it just felt . . . fake."

Sean goes back to drawing in the dirt. Although there's enough moonlight right here to make out shadows, I can't see the detail in his artwork. I fumble in my jacket pocket for my flashlight and shine it on the ground. He's adding lines to the circle, curves spanning the interior until it looks like a basketball. Next, a stick figure of what I assume is me, hands arched like I'm following up a shot. He doesn't say anything, and neither do I, but the silence is creeping up on me, choking me until the only way I can breathe is if I talk.

114

"My dad has MS," I blurt out. "Do you know what that is?"

Sean stops drawing and gives me a slow nod.

I keep talking, the words that I've held in my mouth for so long rolling along like pebbles in the nearby river. "Then you know what it does. It takes your life away. He used to be this athlete—he played ball in college and does rec leagues. Or, he did. Now he can't do much besides shoot baskets. And even that will probably change and soon he won't . . . he won't . . . be doing any of it. Which everyone in my family seems to be ignoring. And he knew. About his MS. My whole family knew and kept it from me. Like I'm some little kid who needs to be protected." I stop to brush the tears away. Oh my gosh. I'm full-blown crying in front of Sean. I bury my face in my hands, hoping to shield myself from the mortification.

"Keep going," Sean says gently.

I look up at his face, which is soft and earnest and kind. I swallow. "So part of me feels like I need to stop sports because he can't do them, but this other little piece of me is trying to hurt him. Which is awful, I know it's awful. But if I'm not mad, then what am I? What do I feel then?"

I sniff and wipe my eyes on my jacket. That late-night bird chirps again and I contemplate chucking a rock at it. When the irritating lullaby ends, Sean rests his hand on my knee for a moment so brief, I'm not even sure it happened. He stands and picks up my bike.

"This bike really is a joke, you know that?" he asks.

"Whatever. It was expensive."

Sean snorts and kicks the tires. "First off, it's a mountain bike. The gears suck and it's heavy. If we're going to have you riding more, I'll have to get you my old road bike. It should fit you if I lower the seat." He rubs his chin. "And that helmet, well, maybe you can borrow Grady's. It's too bad it's supposed to snow again this weekend, but it might be good to get you into a spin class first to get you in shape before spring. I'm not sure the team will—"

"Hello!" I wave the flashlight beam in front of his face. "I'm not a *cyclist*."

"Not yet."

I put my hands on my hips. "And why the sudden need to go into this right now, after I bare my soul to you. Trying to change the subject?"

Sean blinks. "I know about MS. I've done a lot of rides and runs for it—for all sorts of diseases. For the last two years, I've done a ride called the City to Shore. Starts near Philadelphia and ends in Ocean City. Obviously, you won't be able to do the whole thing, but you can do part of it. Maybe 25K."

"How does me riding a bike have anything to do with MS?"

"You get sponsors and donations and the money all goes to MS research. And you can ride for someone you know. Last year I biked for this guy my mom sold a house to. Really got to know him and I felt like . . . like I was doing something right. So I think if you commit to this, it could help you with everything you just talked about. You might not be able to make your dad better, but you can still help."

"How do you know I want to?"

"Well, don't you?" he asks.

I avoid his gaze by shutting off the flashlight and stuffing it back into my pocket. How did this conversation balloon so out of my control?

"Or are you going to keep moping about it?"

I grab the handlebars of my bike from Sean. What a punk! I tell him all that stuff and he shoves it back at me. "I am not moping!"

"You're totally moping." He pulls the bars back. "But it's cool—you're entitled to a mourning period. Maybe now is a good time to get over it. For your dad. Look, that guy I rode for had a much more advanced stage. He found out and boom, three months later he couldn't walk. So if your dad isn't like that, if he's still trying to play basketball and stuff, then I say take advantage of what time you have, you know?"

Heat rises to my cheeks. "It's none of your business," I say, trying to pull my bike but Sean keeps a firm grip.

"I think you just made it my business," he says.

I tug on the seat of the bike and try to yank it away but it doesn't budge. Sean's just watching me with this weird look on his face, like he's amused and sad at the same time.

"Let go."

"No. I mean it, let me help. You still have a choice here."

"Stop."

I ease up a bit on my grip. When Sean does the same, I give one more firm tug. Sean is not holding on as tight and my momentum throws him off balance. The bike flies on top of me, along with Sean.

We're face-to-face, with nothing between us but the middle bar. I can see his scar so clearly now, see how deep it really is.

I want to run my fingers over it, to feel the mark that has made such an impression on his life. He makes no effort to move, just stares intently into my eyes.

I'm not sure what is supposed to happen next. The whole thing is too bizarre. One moment I'm admitting more to him than I've admitted to myself. Then we're fighting, and now he's close. The closest he's ever been. And up close like this, with the moonlight turning his hair almost an iridescent white, I think for a moment I wouldn't mind being even closer to Sean Griswold.

I have no idea what Sean is thinking because, like me, he hasn't moved. He isn't leaning in, but he's not moving away. Definitely not moving away.

He's still staring. Into my eyes.

The only movement either of us makes is to breathe. Until we hear a twig snap in the distance, at which time Sean scrambles up and lugs the bike off me.

"Told you your bike is too heavy." He chucks it on the ground.

Jac stomps around the path, Mark in tow on his cell phone. Her arms are crossed and her brow is furrowed.

"Grady okay?" Sean asks, brushing dirt off his shirt.

Jac flips her hair. "Grady is just *fine*. We would have been here sooner but Mark's *girlfriend* called." She grabs my wrist and lowers her voice. "That's right. His girlfriend. Here he is flirting with me the whole time and then this chick calls and he turns to mush. And I have to sit and talk to Grady the Goth the whole time, who is just as charming one-on-one as he is in a group. Where does Sean *find* these people?"

"Tell Caroline I say hi," Sean says to Mark, before turning to us. "I'm surprised it took that long for her to call him. She's got him on a leash."

Mark gives Sean a dirty look. "Stop it," he says. "No, not you, sweetheart. No, I'm not talking to a girl, I—"

Jac rolls her eyes and smiles at Sean. "Well, should we get these bikes down the path? That was so impressive how you handled everything." She squeezes his elbow. "Smart and cute all in one package, right, Payton?"

"Whatever," I grumble.

Sean gives her a goofy grin and shrugs. "Well, I try."

"And I think present company would agree that you succeed." Jac nudges me. I can't tell if she's flirting with him or trying to flirt on my behalf. I step away.

"Um . . ." Sean's grin gets wider. "Thanks."

There he is, just eating up Jac's . . . Jacness only two minutes after whatever just happened . . . happened between us. Seriously, what *did* just happen? My head hurts. I grab my bike and ride it down the path as fast as I can.

"Hold up," Sean calls. "We're coming too."

"No worries," I yell back. "I'll meet you down there."

I pump my legs, not even bothering to clip my helmet straps. I have to get far away so I can think and not listen to Sean's reactions to Jac's stupid flirting.

Once I'm alone in the darkness, I consider the possibility: maybe that whole thing back there was progress. Maybe Sean wants the same thing I do. Now I just have to figure out what that "thing" is.

FIFTEEN

I never used to understand the expression "float through the day." People don't float. They stand. They walk. Maybe run. Feet leave the ground for a moment, but not indefinitely. But somehow, I find myself floating.

I talk to Trent when he drops me off at school. I pretend to listen to Jac as she details her sister's new tattoo. I take notes in math, more scribbles and abstractions than anything legible. Because I'm not there. I'm back on the hill with Sean.

I've never liked a boy before. I've thought boys were cute and I've had crushes, but I've never gone beyond that to the Land of Like. I'd seen Jac go through it so many times and it seemed like so much effort: the doodled notebooks, dissected conversations, trying to look good for that person all the time. I'd rather use energy like that on basketball or something. But now basketball is gone, and here I am.

Was Sean going to kiss me? If not, did he want to? Did he

feel any differently about me now than he did a few weeks ago? What did he think of Jac? Did Jac like him too? Should I tell Jac I like him? Do I like him?

Obviously, in Like Land, all sentences end in a question.

PFE
February 12
The pros and cons of Turning Your Focus Object into Your Crush

Pro: I've gotten to know him better lately, and for the most part, I like what I've learned.

Con: I've gotten to know him better because he's my FOCUS OBJECT and thus, I should maintain a safe distance. I mean, it'd be like that gorilla lady falling for one of her apes. Ew, never mind, it's not like that at all.

Pro: I feel like he knows what I'm thinking, like he understands things in a way no one else does.

Con: I'm not at a point right now where I want someone, least of all a crush, to know what's going on in my head. I don't even want to know what's going on in my head.

Pro: He suggested I do that bike ride for my dad. I'm not sure if I will, but it shows he's a problem solver.
Con: What if I'm one problem that can't BE solved?

Pro: He really is cute. Nice body, nice features, nice . . . niceness.
Con: He really is cute! How can I focus on focusing with all his cuteness distracting me?

Pro: Sean has confidence without cockiness. He's funny, smart, sarcastic, and interesting.
Con: Crap. I've got nothing.

I work on my chart all through biology. Miss Marietta explains our cell project, and since I plan on recycling Trent's (another act of rebellion; I'm on a roll), my fuzziness is more justified. When she faces the board to draw a diagram, Sean turns around.

"Hey," he whispers.

"Hey." I tuck my Focus Journal underneath my biology book.

"Doesn't Miss Marietta kind of look like Jerry's girlfriend in episode 165? The one who walks around naked all the time?"

I look at Miss Marietta and stifle a giggle. "Do you think they're related?"

"Hope not." Sean smiles. "The nudity thing might be hereditary."

This time the laugh escapes and Miss Marietta stops talking. "Do you find the nucleus entertaining, Miss Gritas?"

"Yes. I mean, no. I mean . . . sorry."

She goes back to lecturing and Sean gives me a wink. Usually, winking is something my sicko uncle does after he compliments my "blossoming." I'm not usually a fan of the wink. But Sean's wink says a million things all at once. The fuzzy floating feeling returns, but this time with a scent of peppermint and tire rubber.

A piece of paper hits my head and I look around, confused. Jac's giving me the eye, so I pick up the note and read.

Hey, what were you two just talking about?

I make eye contact with her and mouth, "*Seinfeld.*"

She shakes her head and scribbles on another sheet of paper. She launches and I catch it just before Miss Marietta looks up suspiciously. I'm all innocence as I unfold the paper under my desk.

Research tip/boy tip number one million—even if you <u>say</u> you don't like Sean, it's generally a good idea to avoid the <u>Seinfeld</u> references when talking to boys. No one gets them.

I shrug at the paper, not bothering to look at Jac. She doesn't get it, but Sean does. Sean gets me, maybe even more than anyone else.

My stomach flips at that thought and a haze settles over my float. Sean gets *what I've put out there*, but if he knew the rest, the therapy stuff and the PFEs, he might not be winking my way anymore.

Jac's at least taught me one thing about boys: they don't want a girl with issues. The MS drama makes me high maintenance enough as it is; therapy catapults me into a whole new arena. So I need to convince Ms. Callahan I'm sane or cured or whatever I'm supposed to be so I can get out of these chats.

And make sure that Sean never, ever finds out about my research.

PFE
February 14
Topic: My "I Am Cured!" Speech

Ahem. I've solved Sean's mysteries, and by doing that have explored my own inner child. Or my inner demons. Whatever inner thing I was supposed to look at. Except my innards, because that's just gross.

I shall now continue a normal adolescence consisting of frequent mall visits, vast consumption of Doritos, and countless hours devoted to various Internet addictions. Or something like that.

Okay, maybe I went too far with the inner child part. I'll have to work on it, on my whole show, to really pull the speech off. Part of that is reassessing how I view my Focus Journal. It's not a therapy ploy. It is a regular ol' journal. Which means I'm normal for writing in it. Which means anything I write about a boy should induce no guilt because I'm not using Sean. Girls write notes about boys in journals all the time.

It's required. It's a rite of passage. I really have no choice.

I'm jolted from my speech preparation by the aroma of pancakes and sausage. Mom's new way to promote family togetherness is to exploit my weakness—food. Except I get emotional when I'm hungry, and I can use that to fake-cry better today during the Imposter Dad chat at my counseling session. A few tears coupled with my carefully prepared words and Ms. Callahan will finally, finally proclaim me sane.

I wear a mature and polished outfit—gray skirt and black top—so it looks like I've grown up and transformed. And I match. Progress. I'm looking at myself in my full-length mirror when Trent weasels into the room.

"What's with the outfit? You revolting against Valentine's Day or something?"

I stare at him, the remark not registering. Valentine's Day. I'd completely spaced it. Which meant I'd also spaced on making my trash card.

Trash cards have been a family tradition since Mom and Dad met. The legend goes that they were so poor when they first got married that Dad made Mom's card from things in the trash. The tradition has grown, and now every year we each choose a name, make a card, and vote on whose is the most disgusting. I would, of course, lose this year because I forgot to make Dad's and now had nothing.

"Not revolting." I turn back to the mirror. "I just . . . forgot it was Valentine's Day."

Trent whistles. "Bad news. I'm guessing you didn't do a card, either."

"I . . . just haven't finished it." Which isn't a total lie. My room was littered with trash, so I've already prepared the materials. "But I will. Promise."

"You better. Dad would be crushed if you screwed this up too."

I let out a slow breath. Dad wasn't the only one I had to consider. Jac takes valentines to the craziest degree, especially with me because she's not really feeling the love with anyone at home. I consider doing nothing as payback for the weird flirting the other night, but I doubt she even knew she did something wrong. I haven't technically told her I like Sean—if I do indeed like Sean. And since the only other valentine she'll get is flowers from her dad's girlfriend, today I needed to come through for her. And my dad. And prove my sanity.

I hate this holiday.

I sigh. "I'm not going to screw this up. Look, I didn't get anything for Jac either and we always do something. Take me to Rite Aid before school and I'll make a great card for Dad."

"Fine. I'll take you. For Dad's sake." Trent smirks. "Did you want to get something for your boyfriend from the mall too?"

"Sean? Why would I do that?"

" 'Cuz you snuck out to see him the other night."

My jaw drops. "I . . . I don't know . . . How did you—"

"Please. The whole 'I'm having girl problems' tipped me off. And our rooms are next to each other. But, hey, relax, secret's safe for now. I'll just hold on to it for later."

The weird thing is, the truth kind of liberates me. I've proven

I'm more grown-up than he thought and grown-ups discuss their relationships openly. "Sean's a great guy; maybe I'll get him something. Maybe I'll get something for another guy. And maybe I'll just let them get me something."

Trent laughs. "Man, I miss high school. Okay, let's go buy some teddy bears and plastic roses."

♥ ♥ ♥

After I stock up on valentine goodies, Trent drops me off and I walk into Greystone High. As predicted, heart-shaped balloons fill the halls. Some, no doubt, are self-bought due to the universal teenage belief that without a valentine, you are a loser.

Jac's waiting next to my locker, which is decorated in crepe paper, balloons, and taped-on candy. Is having your best friend be your valentine every year the same as having no valentine at all? She squeals when she sees me and gives me a hug.

"Happy V-Day, sugar-pop! Do you like the deco?"

I grin despite myself and hug her back. She may be a boy-crazy maniac, but she's my boy-crazy maniac. "You've outdone yourself."

"Just wait until you open it."

I rush through my combination and when the locker opens, candy, roses, and a hideous stuffed purple cat spill out onto the floor. Jac grabs some candy and throws it up in air, dancing around and laughing. The hall monitor gives her a weary look and I scramble to clean up the mess.

"Okay, my turn," Jac says, closing her eyes and holding out her hands. "Whatcha get me? Whatcha get me?"

I unzip my backpack and hand her a paper Rite Aid bag. "It isn't much."

Jac looks inside and then at me in bewilderment. "No, it's great. Candy. I like . . . candy."

"It's not just candy." I rummage through the bag's contents. "It's a joke. Think about it. A lollipop, Sugar Babies, honey chews, a box of gumdrops. The can of pumpkin is a stretch but they didn't have an actual pumpkin this time of year."

Her face is still blank. "Oh, um . . . help me out."

"Jac, it's all your pet names in a bag. Lollipop, honey, pumpkin. I couldn't find one for darling, though."

She thinks about this for a moment, then smiles. "Oh, I get it. So it's one of those it's-the-thought-that-counts gifts, right?"

"Never mind. It was a stupid idea. I was just trying to be creative. I should have gotten the teddy bear holding a heart."

"No! I love it." She pops a gumdrop in her mouth. "Gumdrop. Too punny. Get it, PUNny instead of fun—"

"I get it." Her present is better. Mine sucks. Yeah, I get it.

She shrugs. "Well, this is just the start. Wait until you see what I do in biology."

"Nothing embarrassing?"

The bell rings. "I gotta go. See you in bio." Jac skips down the hallway.

"Nothing embarrassing, right?" I call after her.

She doesn't answer.

SIXTEEN

The promise of biology hangs over me all morning. What is Jac going to do? And what'll it be like when I see Sean?

I didn't get him a valentine. I mean, we still hardly even know each other. A love for *Seinfeld* and two little bike rides doesn't make us lovers; it doesn't even make us friends. But then I think about how close we were that night, about the way he looked at me, and figure that even if I can't label what's going on, there is at least *something* going on.

I take a breath before walking into biology and pray Jac isn't dressed up as Cupid. But it isn't that bad. My desk is decorated similar to my locker, with crepe paper and balloons. The bell hasn't rung yet and only a few students, including a smiling Jac, watch as I hurry to clean up her endless valentine. I'm on my hands and knees picking up the Dove chocolates Jac has sprinkled on the floor when I hear Sean's voice.

"What are you doing?"

"Nothing," I answer without looking up. "Just cleaning this mess."

"I know, but why? I don't want it cleaned up."

"Why does it matter?" I finally shoot a glance at Sean's puzzled face.

"Because it's my desk."

I count the seats back to see it is, in fact, the third seat in the second row. Mine is the fourth. I shift my gaze to the first seat in the fifth row and find Jac with her arms folded tightly across her chest. "What are you doing?" she mouths.

I stand up but keep my focus on the ground. "Sor . . . sor . . . sorry. I thought it was my seat."

Sean reads the large pink card. "From your Secret Admirer." He looks around the room and lowers his voice. "Any idea who it can be?"

I look him square in the eye and realize he thinks it's me. He thinks I'm his Secret Admirer. And I can't tell what he thinks about that. He lips are in a tight line and his ears have gone pink. Like he's embarrassed.

His cheeks grow redder and I understand. Sean's too nice. He doesn't like me and now he thinks he has to let me down easy. He's embarrassed, not for himself, but for me.

I can't help it. Tears fill my eyes. I bolt out of the room before Sean, or Jac, can hurt me anymore.

PFE
February 14 third period, from inside the girls'
bathroom
Topic: Confessions from the Valentine Killer

JAC. IS. SO. DEAD.

Seriously. Dead.

I never go back to third period, making this the first time I have ever ditched a class. Instead, I spend the next two periods writing nasty things about Jac on the bathroom door. I write it in pencil so I can erase it when I'm done. I may be angry, but I'm not criminal enough to permanently defile school property.

The school intercom buzzes. "Payton Gritas. Please report to the counselor's office. Payton Gritas."

I finish erasing my handiwork but slam the bathroom door hard behind me as a final act of defiance. Of course the counselor is paging me. Word of my meltdown must have reached every corner of the school. No way can I convince her I'm fine now. I can't even convince myself.

Ms. Callahan is wearing her same lipstick-stained smile when I walk into her office. The smile stays on her face as she asks me to sit down in front of her desk. Maybe it's to cover up her deep sorrow. I am a lost cause. Incurable.

"Is everything all right, Payton?"

"Why, did someone tell you it wasn't?"

"No." Her smile fades into a thoughtful frown. "I was just concerned because you missed our session. I sent a note to your class, but you weren't there. The office said you'd been reported as present. Were you cutting class?"

I realize how tightly I am gripping the arms of my seat,

131

like men in white coats are going to bust into the room at any moment to take me away. My fingers, my whole body relaxes as I realize that this is just like any old session, that she has no idea about Sean or Jac or the valentines.

I can still convince her I am cured.

I lean in. "Stomach problems. You know how it is. But the Imodium I took finally kicked in, so I'll be all right. I should have gone to the nurse, I know, but I was embarrassed. Sorry. I brought my Focus Exercises, though."

"Don't worry about that." She waves her hand in front of her face and stands. "We're doing something different today."

"But, Ms. Callahan, you should read them."

"I don't read your journal," Ms. Callahan says.

"Well, just the last one. Here, I'll read it to you. In fact, I think it'll prove I'm pretty much cured."

"Cured? Payton, this isn't about 'curing' you. And I told you we were trying something new." Ms. Callahan pushes a button on her phone and says, "Georgia, can you send in the next student, please?"

Oh, crap. I bet it's Sean. I curse the day I ever looked at his stupid head. "Ms. Callahan, please tell me you're not bringing Sean in here. The whole focus thing is done. Let's talk about my dad now. Please?"

"Sean? Who's Sean?" There's a knock at the door and Ms. Callahan strides across the room to open it. "You didn't request Sean for your Conversation with Dad."

"You wanted to see me, Ms. Callahan?"

And, of course, standing in the doorway, with a pass in her hand, is my former best friend.

Ms. Callahan's smile stretches to display all her teeth, not just the lipsticked ones but the fillings in back too. Surely she believes her ingenious idea to bring Jac in for a session will land her on the cover of *School Counselor's Weekly. Saved! Young Teen in Denial Helped by Her Best Friend. Special Feature: Counselor of the Year.*

"I don't want her here." I squint my eyes to the point I can hardly see the two of them hovering by the door.

"We talked about this. It's good to have someone close to you here so we can start exploring some deeper issues."

"Whatever." I fix my gaze on the picture of Ms. Callahan's fat cat. Poor thing. We're both her prisoners.

Jac eases into the seat next to me. I don't look over.

"Payton, is everything all right?" Ms. Callahan asks again with a tone of such worry you'd have thought I'd just killed her stupid feline.

I jut my thumb in Jac's direction. "Why don't you ask her?"

"Ask me what? Hey, what was with you in biology?"

"Like you don't know, backstabber."

"Payton!" Jac's voice is shocked. "What's your deal?"

"My deal?" I'm a science-fair volcano, filled with baking soda, and Jac's just doused me with a whole lot of vinegar. "Are you kidding? What is *your* deal?"

"Is this about Sean? Okay, so I should have told you, but then you would have talked me out of it."

"Because you are insane! Why are you giving him a valentine? Why can't you just leave him alone?"

"It wasn't from me. It's from you."

"And that makes it less crazy? Plus, you were totally flirting with him at the park."

133

"No, I was flirting *for you*. And see!" Jac's eyes are triumphant. "See! You were jealous. I knew it. It's so obvious you like him, and just needed a push—"

"A push? All you do is push. You might as well have shoved me off a cliff."

"I can't believe you're acting like this. You should be thanking me—"

"*Thanking* you?"

Ms. Callahan shakes her head. "Now girls, this isn't—"

Jac cuts her off with a bitter laugh. "So I'm supposed to sit and listen to your denial even more? It's bad enough that you won't even discuss stuff about your dad. Now this crap with Sean. 'Jac—he's my Focus Object. Jac—his head is big. Jac—I'm too scared to say what I'm actually thinking.' Give me a freaking break."

"Wait," says Ms. Callahan. "You have a *boy* as a Focus Object?"

I ignore her. "If I said I liked him, you would tell him."

"What is so wrong with that? Why can't you say what you actually feel?"

"Maybe I don't need everyone in my business like you do."

Ms. Callahan stands up and starts pacing. "I don't know what you girls are talking about, but let's steer the conversation to the core here. Payton's father."

"Right. Payton's father. Who is, like, the best dad ever and Payton is so selfish all she thinks about is herself."

I gasp. "You're the one who's selfish! It's like you're trying to take over my life. Sean, counseling, my Focus Exercises, my brother. Seriously, who's the stalker now?"

134

"So I gave Sean a valentine for you." Jac flips her hair violently behind her shoulders. "So what. I was being NICE thinking about someone else. You should try it sometime."

I stand up and point my finger at Jac. "Nice? You're trying to *force* me to talk to a guy when I'm not ready. Gah, like I don't have enough going on at home—"

Jac stands and gets into my face. "Don't even talk to me about family crises."

"Are you serious? My dad has a disease—"

"Oh, boo freaking hoo. At least he's still around!" Jac cries, her cheeks wet with tears. "You want some professional advice? You have the most perfect life and you can't even see it. A friend who goes out of her way to help. Parents who love you and worry about you and book counseling sessions for you. You have it so good, you have to create drama. Walking around wearing your dad's T-shirt like he's dead. He's not going to die, Payton. He's right there. He's right there and you're acting like he's already gone."

"I'm not going to take this. I'm leaving."

"You don't get to make an exit, I do!" Jac yelps as we both lunge for the door. We're there at the same time, clawing at the doorknob. And somehow, we stop clawing at the door and go at it with each other. Jac's hair smacks my face as I try to scratch her neck. She grabs my arm and twists it. I howl. Ms. Callahan somehow gets into the mix, and I think I mistake her shin for Jac's.

"YOUNG LADIES!"

We stop midfight and look at our school counselor, whose normally passable hairdo has poofed to a frightening height. "You will stop this childish behavior at once!"

135

We release each other and look down at the floor, breathing heavily.

"Apologize."

"Sorry, Ms. Callahan," we say in unison.

Ms. Callahan pulls out a compact mirror and begins the hopeless attempt at fixing her hair. "Now to each other."

I cast a sideways glance at Jac. "Sorry," I say. Then, low enough that Ms. Callahan, who is now smearing her lips with lipstick, doesn't hear, "Sorry you're crazy."

Jac smiles sweetly. "Sorry," then adds in an equally low voice, "Sorry you're a crazy selfish—"

Ms. Callahan snaps her mirror shut. "I think that's enough for today. I'll be contacting your parents about your actions and scheduling . . . separate sessions. We're done."

Jac and I slip out of the office. We give each other a hard look before going our separate ways in the hallway. Ms. Callahan is right about one thing.

We're done.

SEVENTEEN

There's no point in going to class now. The teacher would see the state I'm in and send me right back in for counseling. Instead, I continue walking in the opposite direction of Jac. It doesn't matter which direction, as long as it's not hers.

I can hardly even see where I'm going, my eyes are so blinded by rage. I finally stop in a random hallway and slide down a wall. Jac is so out of line. She has not only ruined our friendship, but ruined things with Sean. She's just a big fat . . . ruiner. And a liar. Me? Selfish? Come on. I'm the one always living in her wake. I'm the one with parents who neglected to tell me about my dad's disease. Yeah, okay, so her family situation is less than ideal, but how was I supposed to know it still bugs her? She's always bragging about her mother's leniency and her sister's partying. I thought she was over it.

When Jac's dad left, I was right there giving her exactly what she needed. A little kick in the pants. Some consistency. I made her hang up the phone when she tried pranking his girl-friend. I threw out the Heineken she stole from the nearby

Wawa. I told Josh Henderson she had mono so he would stop jamming his tongue down her throat every time they saw each other. Me. Wholesome. Kind. Thoughtful.

There's a little voice in my head telling me I'm being unfair. Jac never said anything when I quit basketball. She listened to me rant and rave about my parents. She never made fun of the whole therapy thing and "researched" with me. She was there for me in a different way. I was her drill sergeant. She was my cheerleader. I shudder at the thought that maybe there was truth to Jac's words. Maybe I am just being a selfish brat. But I silence it by pressing my hands firmly over my ears. This is my pity party, and the voice of reason is not invited.

"What are you doing?"

Hands still firmly planted over my ears, I look up to see Grady, crutches and all, peering down at me. A large black case is propped between his right leg and the crutch.

"Sitting. It's a free country."

Grady whistles. "Simmer down. I'm just trying to get into my locker. You didn't trade back, did you?"

I take in my surroundings for the first time. My subconscious connection to my old locker must have brought me here. Of course I'm in the Hall of Terror. Of course I stumble into the most hateful place on campus on a day that I should be feeling nothing but love. Where is the *love*?

"Sorry." I stand up. "Do you need some privacy to perform your live sacrifices? Is that your torture kit in there?" I point at the black case.

Grady actually smiles. I think it's a smile. It's a different expression than his usual sinister smirk or fang flash. This look

138

almost borderlines on friendly, which, of course, completely freaks me out. "It's my saxophone. And I guess if you don't like jazz, it would be torture." He props his crutch against the locker and eases the case down. After spinning in his combo, he shoves the case into his locker with his shoulder.

This is why I don't like him. Always sneaking up on me. Biting me on the shoulder, then swinging a jazz instrument around like it's totally normal for someone so . . . non-bandlike to play the saxophone. I wonder if he's in marching band. Does he have to wear those hideous uniforms? That I'd like to see.

"So." He gives his lock one final twist. "Is that why you're ditching class? Mistook my case for something more evil and followed me in hopes you can apprentice me? I can teach you how to disembowel a cat in two minutes."

All sensation leaves my body. "You . . . you really do that?"

"Payton, I'm not a feline killer." Grady coughs. "You really do think I'm psycho, don't you?"

I bite my lower lip and shrug.

Grady stuffs his crutch back under his armpit and hobbles for a moment before gaining balance. "You're the one stalking Sean, and I'm the weirdo."

"Who says I'm stalking Sean?"

"Jac."

I make a mental note to amend my previous Focus Exercise. Death is too kind. Devise torture chamber instead.

"I don't know what you're talking about." I back away.

"Oh, I know all about it. The whole way to my house Jac was trying to brag about how wild you girls are to Mark, so he'd stop talking to his girlfriend and listen. I said you're so uptight and perfect I could stick a quarter up your butt and it'd come back two dimes and a nickel."

"That was sweet of you."

"I only speak the truth. So then, she said you're in therapy and if I read your Focus Journal about stalking Sean, I'd see how cool and twisted you are." He grinned. "She shut up real quick after that. You might want to buy your friend a muzzle."

If I hadn't been mad at her already, such a betrayal of trust would be enough to send me over the edge. Forget torture chamber. Slowly pluck out all her nose hairs. Then make her eat them.

Grady's expression softens. "Relax. Don't get mad at your friend. She was defending you. And it's not my business if you're doing some weird tree-hugger therapy with Sean."

"Thanks for not saying anything."

Grady puts a finger over my lip. His hands are surprisingly warm. "You didn't let me finish. It's not my business, unless it hurts Sean. If you're using him—"

"I promise I'm not." I shake my head until he moves his finger.

"Good. Because he's just as gullible as you. And God knows why, but I think he might be into you."

"He . . . he is? I mean, I'm . . . I'm not. Gullible, that is."

A group of Mohawk-adorned juniors turn around the corner and stop when they see Grady talking to me. He clears his throat. "So when are you going to take off that chastity belt, princess?" They snicker. Grady lowers his voice and adds, "Don't tell Sean I said anything or I'll make sure this little field trip to your old locker is your last."

"I'm so scared," I say, even though I am.

"Don't pretend you're not."

I refrain from sprinting my non-gothic butt out of the hallway. I spoke with Vampire Boy and lived to tell the tale. It's like I've been given a second chance at life. And even better—perhaps the one bright spot to the messy day—is what Grady said to me. That Sean might be into me. Even in goth speak, that's got to mean something.

♥ ♥ ♥

I start Dad's valentine the second I get home from school. My base is a poster board I'd done my seventh-grade history project on. I crumple it up and rip off some of the pictures, making sure to leave scraps of paper hanging and cut it into a sloppy heart. Next, I scribble pink and red marker until only snips of white show through. A big glob of glue is squirted over the entire piece, smearing some of the marker. Then I randomly stick the contents of my trashed bedroom floor around the edges of the heart. A Snickers wrapper, those annoying postcards from my *Consumer Reports* magazine, used mint dental floss, a cracked nail file, and an empty box of contacts. In the middle, I duct-tape a red piece of construction paper for the message I still need to write.

Stepping back, I appraise my artwork. It's trashy, but it needs something really foul, like a blackened banana peel or used chewing gum. All that is left lying around is some torn computer paper, so I head down to the garage to scavenge through the good stuff.

Whoever wired the electronics in our garage did an awful job. The switch is in the top right corner, away from the entrance and far from the door into the house. At night, we have to navigate around boxes and storage bins just to flip the switch. I'm making my way through the darkened jungle when my knee bangs into something. Hard.

"Whatduhheckwasthat!" I fall to the ground and grab my knee. The unidentified object crashes against the boxes and I somehow manage to crawl to the far wall, stand, and flick on the light.

It's a bike. One I've never seen before. It's not like your everyday mountain bike—this one looks more like Sean's, with thin wheels and a metallic frame. Not something you find at Wal-Mart.

Sean. Is it . . . is it Sean's? There's a silver helmet dangling from the handlebar. I take it off and try it on my head. It feels a little lumpy on top, like the straps are attached wrong. I take it off and look inside to find a red piece of paper shaped like a star.

Hey Payton,

Now you're out of excuses. MS 150 ride, here we come.

Happy V-Day,
Sean

P.S. Still a little curious about the secret admirer thing.

The garage door opens and my dad drives in. I shove the card into my pocket, but there's no way the bike will fit in there too.

"Whose bike?"

I look down at it, in shock that it's actually real. "Mine, I think."

"Where'd you get it."

"Uh . . . my friend."

Dad kicks the wheel and whistles. "Must be a really good friend."

"Yeah. Yeah, he is."

Dad raises an eyebrow. "He?"

I nod but don't say anything. Dad chuckles as he disappears into the house.

Along with the helmet, Sean had also added some old bike shoes to the package. They're a little snug on my unusually large feet, but they feel better once I click my feet into the pedals. The bike can't weigh more than a few pounds; it's amazing something that thin can hold all of my weight.

I ease the bike down the driveway and pump my legs up the hill of our cul-de-sac. Sean was right—this has an entirely different feel. I circle around the street, going faster and faster like I'm being flushed down a toilet bowl. When I reach the center of the circle, I break and watch my breath as I gulp in air.

I'm not thinking about my family, or counseling, or Jac, or even Sean. I'm not worried about what's going to happen when I get home, or what happened today at school.

I'm not worried, period. I just feel free.

♥ ♥ ♥

After riding for an hour or so, I go upstairs to finish Dad's card. I consider calling Sean to say thanks, but I'm not sure what I'm thanking him for. Is it a valentine? The bike implies we'll ride together, but maybe it's just Sean being nice. And he did tell me he would loan me a bike for the big MS ride.

The bike ride. Should I do it? Sean sounded so confident when he explained the course—like it really was possible. It would take lots of work to get in shape, but the ride would also be a good goal. My dad would be happy. And it would gua-rantee more time with Sean. I can't mentally commit yet, but it's still worth considering.

I'm almost done writing a silly poem on Dad's card when Mom calls me down for dinner. I cover my trash day card with a pillowcase and cart it down for the festivities. Mom, Dad, and Trent have already lined theirs up on the kitchen table next to the package from Caleb, who we'll call later on the computer so he can watch my face when I open his card. I'm pretty excited—Caleb always goes all out.

I know my family is weird. I already went over how the whole thing started, but somehow over time it's gotten out of hand. The holiday has become consumed by the trash theme. Mom makes gummy worm and "dirt" (crushed Oreos) sundaes. Dad makes us all play love songs on upside-down metallic trash cans. One year, Trent lobbied for us to attend a mud wres-tling match, but that didn't go over well.

My mom brushes past me on her way to the kitchen. "Can you wrap up the fish sticks? I just have to finish the french fries and we can sit down and eat."

"Sure thing. Where's the fresh newspaper?"

"It's on the table."

"Oh, happy Valentine's Day!" I smile.

"You too," Mom says suspiciously.

I get to work assembling newspaper cones for the fish and chips. When I'm done, my mom dumps in the fried mess and we all sit down on the ground to eat.

If you would have told me after The Jac Incident today that I'd be this happy at dinner, I would have laughed. Or, more likely, cried. But I just can't stop smiling. Sean got me a bike. And riding it was the best feeling in the world. And it's fun now, wondering what's happening inside Sean's head, and clinging to the hope that his feelings match my own.

There. Okay. I said it. I'm definitely feeling something for Sean.

"So how was your Valentine's Day, Dad?"

My dad's fish stick freezes midway to his mouth. "It was great. How was yours?"

"Fabulous! Aren't these fish sticks delicious?"

"Did you hit your head?" Trent asks.

"No. Why?"

Dad clears his throat. "This fish reminds me of something."

"School lunches?" I ask.

Dad flashes his irresistible smile and shakes his head. "No, I was thinking more along the lines of where it came from. The ocean."

"Yeah." Trent pops his tenth stick into his mouth. "From the ocean and probably from the farm and maybe even a land-fill. These aren't exactly fresh."

Dad examines his fish stick. "You know, you're right. I think this family deserves some fresh fish."

"Hey," Mom says. "I'm sticking with the theme here. I'll

make you some of that salmon in the freezer later in the week."

"Not good enough. I want something fresher."

"What are you getting at?" Mom asks.

Dad stands up and pulls an envelope out of his back pocket. "I was thinking maybe some swordfish. Or marlin. I hear the marlin is delicious in Florida. Which is why I booked us all a flight to the Keys for spring break. Because this family deserves a decent meal."

My mom squeals and hugs Dad's legs. Trent lets out a whoop and starts singing some rap song about girls in Miami. I pull my knees up close to my chest and don't say a thing. My happy mood has evaporated. I gave this the okay. Too late to change my mind again. The tickets are booked—my family canceling now is about as likely as a Florida snowstorm.

EIGHTEEN

I never realized how much of my day's activities involved Jac until she wasn't there. I mean, she was THERE, at school, but we both made a point of avoiding each other. Like, before school I saw her out of the corner of my eye turn into the hallway. She saw me and turned right around. Meaning she'd have to walk all the way around the portable class-rooms just to get into the adjourning hallway and make it to her class.

I get to bio early, intent to slouch over my math book, making it look like I'm scrambling to finish an assignment and not avoiding Jac. The only one in the room is Miss Marietta, who seems completely oblivious to my presence. Her head is down on her desk again with a halo of stringy hair cascading around her.

This is the fourth time in the last three weeks she's looked like this. She must be quite the partier. Maybe she even does drugs. Can you imagine? A teacher—the person who introduces DARE and all those "Just Say No" school programs—shooting up? I move closer to her desk to see if I can find track marks on her arm. But then she hears me and jumps up in her seat.

"Payton! I didn't realize you were in here. Is it third period already? Where did the prep time go? Ugh, I didn't even finish grading those papers. There goes my lunch."

She says it all in one breath, like it's not a sentence but just one super-long word. And she's not really saying it to me, she's more talking out loud to herself and I just happen to be there. No track marks on her arm, although her eyes are puffy and red, but not hungover red. Crying red.

"Oh. Um . . . Miss Marietta? Is everything all right?"

Her shoulders sag. "Do I look like everything is all right?"

I give what I hope looks like a knowing and sympathetic nod. We are both women of the world. She parties until dawn and I get a valentine from the boy I'm researching. We can understand each other. "I know how it is."

She looks me up and down for a moment and lets out a terse laugh. "I seriously doubt that."

"No. Really. Guy troubles are tough."

She rustles through some papers on her desk and says in a low voice I'm not sure I'm supposed to hear, "Guy troubles. I *wish* all I had to worry about was high school drama."

My classmates start to fill into the room, including Sean and Jac. Although Miss Marietta's assessment that high school drama is any easier than adult problems is *way* off, I still feel like I need to help somehow. I go for her elbow and give it a quick squeeze, unsure if it's too over the line to give a teacher a hug. I don't know why I chose the elbow and not say, her

148

shoulder. Awkward. She gives me a tight smile and takes a step back as if to say I'm dismissed.

"All right, guys. Instead of doing a class review on cell components, let's have you partner up and go over last week's notes. Make sure you cover all the parts of the cell, because that will be on your next test. I'm here if you have questions but . . ." She sighs. "I'm a little tired, so . . . try not to have too many questions."

The room buzzes with everyone partnering up. I search for Sean, figuring this will be a good opportunity for me to ask about the bike. I spot him sitting next to Jac, who is already talking to him a mile a minute. She looks my way just long enough to give me a smug smirk.

So Jac's decided to go for Sean after all. Traitor. I bet she was lying about the valentine being on my behalf. She was probably just moving in. Well, one thing is for sure, I'm not going to let Jac walk all over me like before. I'm taking control from now on.

Their heads are bent low over Sean's notes when I tap him on the shoulder and flash him a smile that would rival my dad's. "Hey, guys. Mind if we study together?"

Jac scrunches up her nose. "I believe Miss Marietta said partners, as in only two. And if you count, you'll see that quota is already full."

"Quota. Wow. Big word."

"I know lots of big words. *Narcissist* is another."

"What's going on? Do you two have a problem with something?" Sean asks, puzzled.

"No." I smile again and pull a seat close to Sean. "I don't have a problem. Jac might have a problem but—"

"I don't have a problem either," Jac says. "Everything is fine."

"Peachy," I say.

"Fabulouso," says Jac.

"Well . . . good." Sean opens his book. "I'm sure it's all right if you study with us. I don't think Miss Marietta would notice." A tense pause follows. Jac looks at the ceiling. I look at the floor. "Um . . . should we look at that one picture on page 285? The one with all the parts mapped out?"

We all exhale at the release in tension.

"Love to," I say.

"Can't wait," Jac says.

"I guess I'll quiz you guys first. Let's see . . . what are mitochondria?"

"Powerhouse of the cell!" Jac and I chime in unison.

"Whoa, you guys are, uh . . . enthusiastic. Okay, so what about Golgi apparatus?"

Jac's face screws up in concentration. My mind rapidly lists off the different vocab words until I come to it. "They're the storage vessels. For waste. Right?"

"Right. I can't believe you remembered that." My reward is a smile from Sean and a dirty look from Jac. I may not know boys, but I sure as heck know the human cell.

The rest of the period proceeds the same way—Jac and I smiling and pushing ourselves closer to Sean, responding to his questions. Sean, switching back and forth between a goofy grin and a baffled frown. And Miss Marietta, head still down on the desk, quiet except for the occasional whimper.

With five minutes left, we've gone through both human and plant cells twice. Everyone else has abandoned all pretense of studying, but Jac and I are neck and neck with the quizzing and neither one is willing to give up.

"Let's do plant parts one more time," Jac suggests, glaring.

Sean fishes through his pocket and pulls out his Advil. "*C'mon*, guys." He counts out four pills. "I think you both know your stuff. You'll do fine, if Miss Marietta ever takes her head off her desk long enough to give us the test."

Jac giggles. "She's kind of a drunk, huh? I hope I'm not like that when I'm old. Partying with some groddy old men."

"She's not old." Sean turns his head and analyzes Miss Marietta. "I'd guess she's twenty-five."

"And she's not a drunk," I say.

"Yes, she is." Jac sticks her tongue out at me. "My sister sees her partying all the time. She's always dancing up on all the guys at the club. I bet she's a slut."

"Your sister would know all about that."

"What did you say?" she asks.

"Just because she looks one way, doesn't mean she's not dealing with something else. Maybe she's super-depressed or her dog died or . . . she just found out she can't have kids. I don't know. There could be a million things wrong with her. So don't you think she's entitled to go out and forget? To like guys and be a little self-centered and do what she wants without worrying about what everyone else thinks? Huh?"

Jac and Sean look like they've been slapped. Jac recovers first and gives a forced laugh. "Gosh, get all serious on us. Hey

151

Sean, you want to study later? I'll teach you everything you ever wanted to know about cell components."

"Sure." He speaks to Jac but he's still gazing at me. "We'll have to do that sometime. Hey, are you okay, Payton?"

Not so much. "I'm fine."

"You want me to walk you to the next class so we can talk?"

Jac's lips melt into a pout. "What about me?"

The bell rings and Sean doesn't answer. It's unclear if he heard her or if he's just choosing not to. He picks up my books and I follow him out the door.

I've never had a boy carry my books before. It's the kind of hallmark you immediately rush to tell your best friend, dissecting the significance for hours. But that's hard to do when you're competing with that friend, she's staring at you and the boy with pure hostility, and you can't figure out why all you want to do at that moment is cry.

"So," says Sean as we navigate our way to the quad. "What's bugging you? You seemed pretty upset a minute ago."

"I'm fine. Everything is great."

"All right . . . but, are you *sure*?"

"I said I'm fine," I snap, then cover my mouth. What is wrong with me?

Sean's eyebrow goes up and his scar arches in unison.

"Sorry. I'm . . . I don't know what is up with me today, but I don't really want to talk about it. Is that cool?"

Sean purses his lips together. "If I said it wasn't, would it matter?"

"No."

152

"Okay. We'll do a change of subject then. Here it goes. Sooooooooo . . ." He draws the *so* out until I giggle. I'm giggling. How does he do that?

"Did you get my bike?"

I stop and slap my forehead. I still haven't thanked him. "Yes! I totally forgot!"

"You forgot? I just gave it to you yesterday."

"No, I mean, I forgot to thank you. I didn't forget about the bike. I love it. I already rode it yesterday."

"Yeah?" Sean grins. "What'd you think?"

"You're right. My old bike was totally slowing me down. This moves much faster. It's like, like I'm—"

"—flying. I know. Isn't it a—"

"—rush," I finish. "Totally. Like nothing I've ever done. It's the best valentine I've ever gotten." I stop, suddenly shy. "I mean, not that it was like a *valentine* valentine. I just mean it was a great gift. If it was a gift?"

Sean blushes. "Oh, yeah. It's just my old bike. You can hold on to it as long as you want. But you better put it to good use."

"I will." We open the doors to the quad and get blasted by a burst of cold. I zip up my coat. "But maybe not for a while. This weather is nuts."

Sean breathes out, his sigh displayed in the frigid air. "I'm disappointed in you, Payton Gritas. You're going to let some weather stand in your way? I thought you were more hard-core than that."

I stiffen. "I am hard-core!"

"No you're not."

"Am too."

"If you were hard-core, you'd come riding with me today."

"I'll not only go with you, I'll bike circles around you."

Sean grins. "Like you did at Valley Forge?"

I screw my face up and try my best to think of the perfect remark. It never comes. The silence turns stale.

"Here, I'll give you a chance to prove your hard-coreness today. I have swim practice, so maybe a little later. Like 3:30?"

"I'll be there," I say. Then, because I want to add something tough I say, "Lamebrain."

Sean lets out a loud guffaw. Half the quad looks our way. "Did you just seriously say lamebrain?"

"I think I did." I raise my chin.

"Is this a word you use often? I mean, should I be offended or flattered or what here?"

"I was trying to think of something hard-core sounding and lamebrain is what came out," I admit.

"Why not buttmunch? I've always been a fan of that one. Even though I have no idea what a buttmunch is."

"I think it's self-explanatory."

"Then that is pretty low . . . Hey. It looks like the school guidance counselor is trying to get your attention."

Ms. Callahan is waving at me from across the quad, the billowing lime green sleeves of her dress flapping like a flag. I instantly look at my shoes, hoping she'll follow the social rules of public ignoring. But—surprise—she's next to us in a minute. Apparently women who wear lime green are unaware of social rules. "Payton, I called your house last night to discuss the . . . incident in my office. I realize it was a holiday so perhaps not the best time but I do plan on contacting your parents in the near future. Maybe even have them come in—"

"Yeah. Yeah that's fine. But can we maybe talk about this *later*?" I give what I hope is a meaningful look. The lady can't be that clueless.

"Oh." She looks from me to Sean and her eyes widen. "Oh! Yes. So this is . . . your friend. I understand."

Yep. She is that clueless.

Ms. Callahan analyzes Sean. "I understand *completely*."

"That's debatable," I say through clenched teeth.

She looks me dead in the eye. "We need to talk."

"Later." I pull Sean away.

"What was that all about?" Sean asks once I've gotten us to safety.

Somehow, she-knows-who-you-are-because-she-just-figured-out-I'm-focusing-on-you doesn't seem like a reasonable explanation. I look down at my watch-less wrist. "Oh, look at the time. You really should get to class. But I'll meet you at Valley Forge around 3:30, 'kay?"

"Yeah, but why did she look at me like that?"

"Bye!" I rush across the quad, staring at my feet some more and willing myself to melt into the floor.

PFE
February 15
The drama that is my life: distributed into a
pie chart

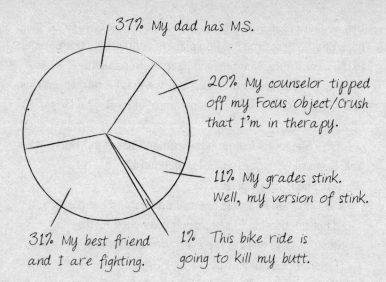

37% My dad has MS.

20% My counselor tipped off my Focus Object/Crush that I'm in therapy.

11% My grades stink. Well, my version of stink.

31% My best friend and I are fighting.

1% This bike ride is going to kill my butt.

NINETEEN

I hardly recognize Sean, he has on so many clothes. Not that I'm much different; I have on thermal underwear, some tight-fitting sweats, a sweatshirt, and my yellow North Face jacket. Ears, hands, and neck are all covered in the appropriate accessories, and yet I still feel like a human Popsicle.

"Warm enough?" Sean asks.

"I'm on the beaches of Hawaii as we speak."

"Me too. Swimming in a lava pit."

" 'Cause we are hard-core."

"To the core," Sean says.

"Well, buttmunch, I'm going to show you how hard-core I am on my new bike here."

"You're drafting?"

"Uh, is that where I bike ahead of you?"

Sean laughs. "Follow me, Gritas. And try not to freeze."

Sean curves his bike down a little hill, taking us in the opposite direction we went last time. He's being cruel, because now we start the ride with a constant, butt-burning incline. I don't say a word, just grip my handlebars and follow. Follow and don't freeze.

His bike makes all the difference. Although my legs protest after only a few minutes, I'm able to keep up at the quicker pace he's set. We reach a point of release by Defender's Gate and coast down until we hit General Washington's headquarters. Sean waves for me to follow him and turns into the parking lot.

"Let's take a break."

I unclip my helmet and pull off my beanie. "Are you kidding me? We've only been going for a few minutes."

"Well excuse me, Miss Hard-Core, but I need to take a trip to the Little General's room."

"Huh?"

"The bathroom, Payton. I have to use the bathroom."

He unclicks his shoes and helmet and walks over to the small building that holds the ticket booth and restroom. I get off my bike and wheel it to an empty bike rack before doing the same with Sean's. The whole parking lot is empty. There are some deer across the field, watching me. I wave my arm, jumping up and down so they'll run away, but deer here are like dogs. Pet one and it won't even stop chewing the grass.

I walk down the pathway and sit on a wooden bench outside the restrooms. There's a sign hanging on the ticket booth window: CLOSED FOR REENACTMENT. As if to confirm it, there's a distant shout of a cannonball. I shudder. Maybe we aren't as alone here as I thought.

Sean comes out wiping his hands on his jacket. "I have a

confession. I'm not hard-core. That water in there is freezing. I think I'm about to wuss out."

I wag my finger at him. "The general would be disappointed in you. Picture doing that bike ride barefoot."

Sean looks around. "I feel like we're on the fourth-grade field trip again."

"The one where the guide kept telling us we should at least be grateful for our jackets?" I ask.

"And shoes."

"And frozen peanut butter sandwiches."

"Remember that hardtack he made us eat?"

I laugh. "I spit mine out in my hand."

"It's like episode 114 where Jerry hides his mutton in his coat pocket," Sean says.

"And Elaine puts it on!"

"And the dogs start chasing her!"

"Classic."

"Yeah." Sean's eyes fill with mischief. "You know what I always wanted to do on that field trip?"

"What?"

"Pretend I was one of Washington's guards. Their bunks are over here." His long legs stride across the small clearing and hop over the wooden fence. I look around for a place to put our helmets and end up leaving them on the bench. I'm not as quick or as sure-footed as Sean—I still have my bike shoes on. He moves in them like they're running shoes and not covered in cleats.

When I finally catch up, he's already ducked under the chain with a DO NOT ENTER sign and is lying down on one of the wooden planks that served as the soldier's bed. I turn back around and survey the vast and lonely park. There's no one else there. No one can see us. With a little thrill, I crawl under the chain and crouch in the middle of the guard's quarters.

The room can't be much bigger than my parents' master bath. There's a crude fireplace on one wall and four thin bunk beds. The quarters have a little desk in the corner with some old canteens and an inkwell on display. A fake Revolutionary War uniform is carefully laid out on the right bunk, like the soldier went to take a bath and never made it back to get dressed.

"This is so cool," Sean says.

"Couldn't we get in trouble for being in here?"

"No, I think the DO NOT ENTER sign is just for looks."

"Oh, right."

Sean pats the weathered board and smiles. "But we're hard-core, remember?"

I laugh and sit primly on the edge of the bed, lowering my head a little so I don't hit the board above me. "I think you might win that contest after all. Breaking the rules freaks me out. And I think I'm literally about to freeze my butt off."

"That would be a tragedy."

"Yeah, well, I've got plenty of it to lose."

"I wouldn't say plenty." He scoots back, giving himself full rein to blatantly check me out.

My mind and heart race. He just gave me a line. A total, flirty line! I avoid his gaze, unable to match him. "That's because you're too nice."

"I'm not that nice."

After a few beats, Sean clears his throat. "You know, when it got really cold, soldiers used to have to spoon all night."

"Spoon?" I ask.

"Lie down, I'll show you."

"Uh—" I run my finger along the board, leaving a mark in the dust.

"Oh, come on. We're just doing a mini reenactment."

He pulls my arm and I'm suddenly facing him, lying down. "Now roll over," he commands.

"What am I, a dog?"

"No, you're a Revolutionary War soldier and you're about to freeze to death if you don't do what I say."

I roll over. Sean scoots closer.

"Soldiers used to lie in rows when they were out on the battlefields and their uniforms were thin from wearing them forever. They'd pull their blankets over themselves and lie all in the same direction. Then someone would call out which direction to spoon and they'd all roll over together. They'd do it all night."

Sean's body is pressed up against mine and I'm surprised I'm even able to assess his historical claim. "But these guys weren't on a battlefield. This is Valley Forge. They all had these cabins."

"So I get my history facts a little muddled. It might have been the Civil War, actually." He scoots a little closer. "It's really just my trick to get warmer."

We lie there for five minutes, not talking, just breathing in unison. There are about ten layers of clothes separating us, but I can still feel his chest muscles push against my back. His left arm is around me and I can feel the muscles in his forearm too. I want to push his jacket back and look at his arms, at his muscles. I want to see if his arm hair matches the hair on his head. It's all for research, I tell myself again and again. I never want the research to end.

"You know what else soldiers used to do?" Sean asked.

"You sound like our fourth-grade tour guide."

"Be nice or I'll make you eat more hardtack."

"No, Mr. Griswold," I say. "What else did Civil War soldiers used to do?"

"Revolutionary War."

"Anyway . . ."

"They played games," he finished. "All different kinds. Card games. Dominoes. Chess."

"Let me just pull out an old Chutes and Ladders from under this bunk and we'll go at it." I strain my neck so I'm peeking under the bed.

He laughs and pulls me back up. "Don't you know any other games?"

"All I know are cheesy car games my mom and brothers used to play."

"Favorite one?"

I squint at the weathered beam above our heads. "License plate bingo."

"Favorite one that we can pretend fits into the American Colonial Era?"

"What about Three Things? My family made it up, it's kind of like Two Truths and a Lie but tweaked."

"What're the rules?"

162

I turn around and face him. His lips look really soft this close up. "They're simple. You say three things about yourself. One is true, the other two aren't. You want to make them all similar, so it's hard to know which one. Then, the other person has to guess. If they guess it right, they get to ask you anything they want. If they guess it wrong, you get to ask them anything you want."

"So then it ends up being like Truth or Dare?"

"People end up streaking in Truth or Dare. This is a family game."

"Got it. I'm in. You go first."

I close my eyes and think. I used to suck at this game because of my lack of scandals. Trent would always lay out three wild stories, stumping us because we couldn't believe one was actually true. Like cow tipping and hang gliding and throwing up on his prom date. After endless car rides, I finally nailed my strategy. Kill them with monotony.

"Okay. Things I did today. First—I filed my nails. Second—I ate watermelon. Third—I put on mascara."

"You're kidding me. You could have done all those things."

"That's the game. One is true, the others aren't. Pick your poison."

Sean chuckles and shakes his head. "All right. I'm going to guess the mascara one."

I groan. "How did you know?"

"Well, watermelons are out of season. Why would you care about your nails when you're wearing gloves, not to mention I always see you picking at them. And your eyes look pretty today." He blushes. "Not that they don't usually. Never mind. I just guessed."

Pretty? My murky brownness pretty? Did he really just use that word? On me? This game is awesome. Awesome. Awesome. Awesome.

"So you got it right. Ask your question."

Sean recovers quickly. "Easy game. So, what was with you and Jac today in biology?"

"Can't you give me another question?"

"Sure. Why was Ms. Callahan looking at me all funny?"

Man. I have to tell him. He's too smart. And I'm too bad at keeping a secret. Plus it'd be breaking the rules of the game not to spill. I'd already reached my rule-breaking quota for the day.

"Jac and I got in a fight."

"Obviously. Why?"

"Well, I'm not exactly sure. She came into my counseling session and—"

"Counseling session?"

Even with the cold, I feel my face heat up. "Oh, yeah. I have to go to these counseling sessions. Because of my dad," I add lamely.

"Got it," he says. And he does. Get it, I mean. Because he doesn't question or pry. And the silence encourages me to go on.

"So she came into my counseling session and I was mad at her for making you that secret-admirer stuff."

Sean sits up and bumps his head on the top bunk. "Ouch!"

"You okay?" I touch his forehead.

"That hurt."

"Well, yeah. It would."

"Not that. Well, *that*, but what you said. *Jac* was my secret admirer?"

164

I pull my hand away. "Um . . . kind of. Yeah."

"Oh. So . . . so it wasn't . . . it wasn't you?"

"Um, no. Jac says she did it for me, but I didn't know she was going to do it."

"So you never got me a valentine?"

"Right. I, er . . . sorry. I should have, I would have, but no. No, I didn't."

"Humph." Sean grunts and lies back down.

"But that's why Jac and I got in a fight. You see, ever since . . . a while ago, Jac has been butting in."

"Butting into what?"

"What? Oh, um . . ." Can I give him the truth without telling him the whole truth and nothing but the truth? He knows about my dad and the sessions. He knows about Jac. But the PFEs and Sean stalking? Forget about it. I have to maintain some semblance of sanity. "Butting into my business. I mean, that part isn't important. She knew how I felt about you and gave you that present without telling me first. That's why we fought. That's my truth."

A goofy grin spreads across Sean's face. "How you felt?"

"Hey, no more questions."

"Fine. But is that really the truth? All of it?"

"Of course." I swallow. "Why would I lie?"

"I just thought it was weird the way Ms. Callahan looked at me today. Like she knew stuff about me. But if she witnessed a catfight in my honor, I guess it makes sense. Although—"

"Your turn," I say. "Three things."

"Three things." Sean strokes his chin. "Let's see . . . First, I am an alien from the planet Xerox, where everyone is a clone. Second, I am secretly a celebrity doing research for my next historical drama in which I star as a dashing guard to General Washington. And third . . . I'm completely, utterly, and overwhelmingly . . . cold."

"Sean! That's obvious."

"That I'm a celebrity?"

"Three." I punch his arm. "But no more freebies like that."

Sean raises his arms to shield himself from further blows. "I can't believe you guessed it. So what's your question?"

My mind goes blank trying to think of a confession. I want to know so many things. Was this whole hang-out-in-the-bunks thing planned out? Did he think I was nuts? What did he think about Jac's stunt? What does he think about me? I can't condense all the thoughts and feelings into one question. I just can't. "What's your favorite color?"

Stupid! What are we, in kindergarten here?

"Green." He coughs. "That's the crappiest you-can-ask-me-anything question I've ever heard."

I sigh. "I know."

"Tell you what. I'll answer the question you should have asked. Ready?"

"So it's like *Jeopardy!*?" I ask.

"Yes. Now, the answer is . . . you," he says.

"Me? Wait, what's the question?"

"Who do you like?"

"Who do I like? Oh, wait. You mean . . ." I stop and look away, too embarrassed to finish the sentence.

Sean lifts my chin and looks me straight in the eye. "Answer:

You, Payton. I like you. For a while actually, but especially lately. Since, for whatever reason, I've gotten to know you better. Good question?"

"Yes. It is."

"Can I tell you three things I want to do right now or should I just show you?" he whispers.

"Show," I answer, blessing the sunny day ten years ago when my mother introduced this glorious game. We were in Maryland. Or maybe Virginia. Regardless, it beat the heck out of license plate bingo. I hold my breath and close my eyes, wondering what the first thing—the THING I've waited for since that first bike ride, since the first conversation, since I set my sights on his head—will be like. I take a peek and see his eyes are closed too. But his mouth is right there and—

"Excuse me."

We open our eyes, look at each other to confirm the other wasn't talking, then turn to the doorway. There's a flash of light and we sit up quickly, simultaneously bumping our heads once again on the too-low bunk. A short and squat Revolutionary War soldier peers down at us, flanked by a family of tourists, one of which continues to take our picture.

"You kids know this is a national park?" asks the soldier. His forehead is bandaged and he's not wearing shoes. He brings new meaning to *hard-core*.

"Yeah, we were doing a reenactment," Sean says.

The soldier spits and the family—mom, dad, and four girls in BEN FRANKLIN INVENTED IT sweatshirts—all take a step back. The littlest one finally puts her camera down.

"What kind of reenactment is that?" asks the soldier.

Sean looks at me with his dorky grin. "Spooning."

♥ ♥ ♥

Mom shows up around the same time as Sean's mom. I wish I had a video camera to document our different reactions. I see my mom walking up and say, "Great. My mom's here."

I expect a sympathy nod from Sean but he's looking past my mom. He stands. "Great! My mom's here!" And he runs up to her and hugs her. How many fifteen-year-old guys hug their moms? In public, nonetheless.

Then Mrs. Griswold starts complimenting the park ranger on his stiff Smokey the Bear hat and before you know it, they're discussing the real estate market. Mom's quiet through it all, fuming and shaking her head. Probably debating which military school to send me to.

Luckily, the park ranger's home is for sale. He begrudgingly lets us go after Sean's mom offers him a seller discount. Sean is still smiling, and there is nothing guilty or sheepish about it. It's like he's happy this is all happening. What happened inside the little cabin, yeah—that is good stuff. But the whole we're-so-about-to-get-it waiting period? Not so much.

The park ranger walks back to his little ticket booth and Sean's mom puts her arm around her son. "You little hellion. It's about time you got into some trouble." She turns to my mom. "I was starting to get worried about him. Thought he'd never act like a normal teenager. He's usually out volunteering or training for his silly sports." Sean flinches. "But mischief is so good for their overall development. I'm glad your daughter helped him explore himself better."

Mom's eyes widen. "Yes, well, Payton has given us plenty of teenage behavior lately. Although I should hope"—she gives us both a stern expression—"not much exploration, by either of you, was happening in there." And without saying good-bye, she turns and marches to her car.

"I'll get your bike for you," Sean says softly.

"Oh, yeah. Thanks."

Sean's mom claps. "This is just too cute. Really, Sean, what took you so long? Now, let us skittle-skattle. I'm showing a home at five."

She whips a cell phone out and Sean's smile wavers. She's done with him.

"Well, see ya," he says.

"Yeah—I guess—"

"Sean! Grab these bikes. Let's not wear out our welcome."

Sean jogs over to the bikes, and I turn and trudge to Mom's car. Sean's mom glorifies our rebellion, then forgets about it minutes later. Not my mother. I am walking on the same ground as some of history's bravest men. Yet I couldn't help but believe, given the choice between facing the British and my mother, they would have taken the redcoats any day of the week.

I let out a deep, icy breath before opening the door of my mom's Dodge Caravan. The heat is blasting full force, but any warmth felt is instantly extinguished by one fierce maternal look.

Mom doesn't say a word for the rest of the night—my own taste of the silent treatment. The silent treatment led to the counseling sessions. This led to me researching Sean. Which led to today's bike ride. If this is the worst she can do, I'd take it every day. It would take a pretty severe punishment for me to regret my crime. I mean, what if that park ranger had only come in five minutes later? He might have found me kissing Sean Griswold. The very same Sean Griswold who proclaimed his unyielding love for me! Or, at least, said he liked me. In a round-about way.

Who'd have thought when this whole mess started that it would lead me to this point. It's like having a tornado wipe your house away only to discover it was built on an oil well anyway.

♥ ♥ ♥

Sometimes my parents forget my room is right next to theirs. Otherwise, why would they always have these deep conversations that I can hear so easily? All I have to do is sit in my walk-in closet and press my ear up against the grate. And I don't even feel bad about it since it seems to be a recurring theme in our family to exclude me from all major conversations.

I grab my dad's Sixers shirt and ball it up into a pillow to listen. My mom can be a major rager. She doesn't do it very often, but when she does, she's like a pop bottle that has rolled around in a car for a few days. When you factor in all the drama with my dad, and me fizzing her up, it's quite an explosion. I don't even need to listen hard to hear her. The neighbors can hear her.

I didn't fully comprehend my mother's anger earlier because I didn't know how much damage had been done. Turns out, the park bit isn't the meat of it. Ms. Callahan called my mom, told her about the Jac fight and then, just to vanquish any doubt that she is deliriously brainless, asked Mom how I was coping with my grades. So Mom was already sitting at the computer checking my report card, stewing at my massive lie, when she got a phone call from an irate park ranger threatening to press charges against her promiscuous daughter.

All that anger, all this yelling, and I don't even flinch. But when she's done, after she's taken a few breaths and asks, "Well, aren't you worried? She shows a complete lack of respect for authority. She lies about her report card. And who knows what she was doing with that boy. If he's anything like his mother—"

Dad cuts her off with a sigh. "I'm just too tired to think about it right now. I have no clue what's going on with her. Let's sleep and maybe I will have the energy to try to figure her out tomorrow."

I lie down in my closet and just listen to myself breathe for a while. I don't know why I've gone through so much energy to close myself off from my parents. It seems just being myself is alienating enough.

TWENTY

The sky opens up and buries the whole Northeast in relentless snow. As a kid, my favorite thing was looking out the window and seeing the never-ending frozen blanket. Snow back then meant sledding and hot chocolate and TV marathons. But today, it's wasted. It's Saturday, so no break from school. And no chance of sneaking out and biking over to Sean's. Even worse, I have an entire day trapped in the house with my still-hostile mother, who wakes me up at the evil hour of 6:00 AM.

"Out of bed now!"

Well, I guess the silent treatment is over. Sadly enough.

I roll over and face the wall. "Saturday."

"Well, I'm going to the Y and you're coming with me." She yanks my comforter off me. "I'm not leaving you alone in this house to create more trouble."

"It's six!"

"You can take a nap when you get home. After you do homework."

I'm totally fine going to the Y, but not when it's still dark. I open my mouth and she shushes me. "Yes, I know about your grades. I had a long chat with Ms. Callahan. By the way, you're grounded. And I'm going to start having all your teachers sign off on your assignments. Things are changing around here. We're leaving in ten minutes."

I lie there for a few more minutes before giving up and slipping out of bed. After throwing on an old white tank, some basketball shorts, and shoes, I poke under my bed for my basketball. Then I remember I no longer play basketball and therefore can't shoot hoops. Great. Mom better not rope me into her aerobics crap.

♥ ♥ ♥

The YMCA in our area is not like the YMCA in a Village People song. It has high, exposed-beam ceilings, a whirlpool, and spanking-new exercise equipment. All the trendy moms in the neighborhood hang out there, and mine is no exception. We check in and Mom heads over to her I'm-middle-aged-but-I'm-still-wearing-Lycra aerobics class. She leaves me alone to stare at the spacious gym.

Since it's a snow day, the open basketball court is not exactly "open." Tons of guys, from teenagers to grandpas, are subbing into pickup games. I'm a girl and the youngest one there, but I know I can still hang. Well, two months ago I could hang. The old man with the wristbands and too-short shorts would school me now.

I watch from the bleachers, oozing with jealousy every time

a sneaker squeaks. Too bad it snowed. If I could talk Mom into it, another bike ride might help fill the basketball void.

I slap my hand to my forehead. I'm in a YMCA! There's a whole row of bikes in the workout room. I ditch the gym and jog through the main hallway. A door opens and a mass of sweaty people pour out. They're all in spandex, so I figure they're either leaving a heavy metal concert or they're bike riders. There are ten stationary bikes set up in the small room. A gorgeous twenty-something girl with waist-length black hair and a body created to display at a gym is toweling herself off.

"Excuse me. Is it all right if I ride one of these bikes?"

She stops toweling and shakes her head. "You have to be enrolled in a spin class."

"Oh." My heart sinks. Back to watching basketball. "Okay. Sorry."

She waves a slender hand in front of her face. "No worries. I've got another class coming in now. Why don't you stay? I had a few cancel 'cuz of the snow."

"Oh, I don't know. I've never really ridden on one of these. I don't even know how to get on."

"It's a bike, girl, not rocket science. Take the one in back. I'm Yessica. Yes, Yessica." She lets out a tinkling laugh. "I'll get you set up."

I watch as Yessica adjusts the bike for me, awed by her beauty and graceful manner. A fresh batch of bikers, or spinners as Yessica calls them, fill into the room and claim their bikes. I settle into my seat and smile a little to myself. A few little bike rides and maybe I'll be able to catch up with Sean when the snow melts. The thought of Sean causes my smile to widen into a grin. Yessica makes eye contact and smiles, thinking it's directed at her. I contort my face into a look of concentration. None of the other spinners are smiling.

"Glad you guys could make it through the snow. We're going to start with a little warm-up here so everyone, on your bikes, keep the resistance low and let's get going."

Yessica cranks up the music and we pedal slowly to Sheryl Crow's "I Want to Soak up the Sun." It's no joyride, biking without going anywhere in a room filled with old people. But Yessica is so nice and it beats the basketball torture. The song ends and Yessica stands up on her pedals.

"I'm just going to dim the lights and we'll get this workout started. Remember while we're doing this: Focus. Keep the end in sight. Whatever that end is for you, hold on to it. Deep breath and here we go."

The lights dim until eerie pink neon is the only light source. The already small room closes around me like a closet. The music pulses and it's not Sheryl anymore . . . it's techno. Like in a nightclub. Come to think of it, everyone is in spandex and the lighting is dark enough. I should have borrowed one of Jac's glow-in-the-dark necklaces.

Jac. Never mind.

"Now push it. Come on people, pump up that resistance. Twist it, twist it."

Everyone is pedaling faster now and I follow. There's a little knob below the handlebars that increases the resistance. They're all twisting it again and again, but I'm burning after one little turn.

"In the back!" Yessica barks.

"Me?" I ask.

"Don't talk! Ride!"

"Sorry."

"Get going! Push that wiggly butt of yours into action."

Um, what happened to little Yes I'm Yessica? She's yelling at all of us, cutting into us the second we let up. Not that we can ever let up, because it's song after song of high-intensity beats. Sweat is washing over me in waves, yet I push and pump my legs until the pink neon swirls around me.

"Don't be lazy! Your mothers are lazy! I want to see you WORK! Focus on your goal! Keep that GOAL!"

The only thing I can focus on is my balance. Thoughts of basketball, my mom, or Sean have all deserted me. My mind is too busy communicating with my screaming muscles. But they are silenced by Yessica's urgent command to go harder and harder. Round and round my legs go, each rotation more impossible than the last. I'm completely consumed by the pain, every ounce of attention I have devoted to fighting it. I'm about flop off my bike and surrender to the overwhelming exhaustion when the music slows down. Through the steam and sweat, I see Yessica is back to her bubbly, smiling self.

"You did it! Awesome. Everyone give your backs a little pat. Now, I want you to imagine you're breezing down a boardwalk on a bicycle built for two. You and your lover, just laughing the day away . . ."

She ends the session with a few more songs and granola meditation drills. The class gives a collective sigh when the lights come back on and Yessica gets back to work with her towel.

"Thanks," I pant after everyone else has left.

"Girl, you were working it! I better see you at my six o'clock Tuesday class. You in?"

It would be crazy to go through such torture again. Fortunately for Yessica and myself, crazy is my specialty. And I've just found something new to focus on—leg-wobbling, butt-burning pain. Which beats the heck out of *thinking*.

"Yeah, sure." I finally catch my breath. "I'm in."

TWENTY-ONE

Dear Ms. Callahan,

My mom told me about your meeting and how you both think it's best I discontinue the counseling sessions for a while. <u>A while</u> are the words my mom used. This can mean weeks. Or months. Or forever, that's fine too. Needless to say, I think this is an excellent idea. What I mean is—I defer to your grown-up intelligence. I think we've seen how much progress I've made, and except for that last little Jac hiccup, I think our relationship has led me to true healing.

So, uh. . . I'm going to keep writing the PFEs if that is all right. Don't worry, I'm not getting in over my head. Or anyone else's head for that matter.

Also, I'm biking almost every day now, and that makes me feel more . . . like I'm me again. You'd be amazed how it has improved my focusing abilities. Actually, most of my day is spent . . . focusing.

♥ ♥ ♥

I settle into a routine over the next few weeks. I go to school, where my days are filled with Sean. Sean at lunch (I've moved to the outskirts of his table), Sean at my locker (we don't share it, we aren't THAT type of couple. Not that we've ever said we're a couple. But we're way beyond labels. It's too cosmic of a connection), Sean in class (notes passed, shoulder taps, winks and nods), Sean at home (not IN my home! I'm grounded for a month. I only go to the school and YMCA. No outdoor bike rides, not that I could with the never-ending snowy weather). So it's Sean on the phone or silly Sean texts. And of course, every night, Sean rules my dreams.

I'm filled with Sean, almost to the top, almost to the brink. But even with all of Sean, all the time, there's still the void that is Jac. I stick to my new route around the school, the route that steers me away from Jac's classes. Away from seeing her with all her other friends. Sometimes I can feel her eyes on me in class, but I don't look over. Is she angry still? Upset? Let down? Or does she miss me like I miss her? I've written so many unsent e-mails, picked up the phone so many times. There is so much news to share! All the things we've talked about guy-wise I'm beginning to understand. Those long hours spent grounded should be spent analyzing Sean with her. She's part of the reason we're together. And he's part of the reason Jac and I are now apart.

Ms. Callahan succeeded in her great psychiatric experiment. I have learned to focus. I focus on everything Sean has to say and the way he says it. I focus on Miss Marietta's glazed expression, her robotic movements. I focus on Yessica's shrill voice, demanding more and more of me through each spin class. I focus on my shoes if I ever see Jac across the squad. All this focusing has made it quite practically impossible to focus on the situation at home.

Home. My new strategy started off almost by accident. I came home from school one day and literally ran into my mom in the hallway.

"Oh, hey, Mom."

Mom shifts her laundry basket to her other hip. "How was school?"

Today at school, Sean leaned over to whisper a secret and his smell combined with the warmth of his breath almost made me delirious. "Um, good. All the teachers signed my assignment sheet. It's in my backpack if you want to check it."

"You see? Sometimes you just need a little structure to get through a rough spot."

"Right."

"Everything else all right? Are you getting along with your friends?"

"Of course! Being grounded isn't exactly helping my social life—"

Mom frowns.

"But everything is the same as before," I add. Which isn't a lie. Jac and I still aren't talking. I'm still avoiding everyone but Sean. Same old. "Well, better go get my Spanish homework done. I'm doing another spin class tonight."

My mom breathes a sigh and smiles. She doesn't have to worry. Her daughter is normal and healthy and adjusted. I've played the part well.

It's so easy this way, I don't know why I didn't try it before. I talk to my parents. I talk with Trent. I just don't talk *about* anything. If the conversation ever veers toward more dangerous territory, toward Dad's latest medication or the big spring break plans, I shift my focus to Sean and I'm fine.

Mostly.

TWENTY-TWO

Of course, it's inevitable that Jac and I would eventually be within a few feet of each other. It happens right outside of biology. The bell's about to ring and we're both racing for the door, coming from opposite directions. We notice each other at the same time and freeze right outside the doorway.

"Go ahead," I say.

"You," Jac says.

"Seriously, go."

Jac fixes me with a stare. A mean, awful, hateful stare that almost knocks me right over. I'd started to consider the idea that maybe things between us weren't completely broken, but with a look like that, any hope of future friendship seems impossible.

I can't meet her gaze, but I also don't give in and walk through the door first.

"Fine." I get a chill as she pushes past me. "Ladies first, I guess."

The class bulletin board hasn't changed since Christmas.

Snowflakes float down on pictures of various animals. Miss Marietta's desk is a nightmare, and come to think of it, we still haven't taken the cell-components test. Whatever is up with her, it's probably bigger than a break-up.

I plunk down behind Sean and am instantly warmed by his smile. He leans in and, as usual, his presence, his very *being*, overwhelms me.

"So," Sean says. "I need you to turn in your sponsor money for the MS 150. Or I'll cover you, no worries. And did I tell you they have a party the night before the ride—free food—and then you get to meet all these other bikers . . ."

I zone out, partially because it fringes on Dad territory and partially because I'm staring at Sean's lips and wondering why I haven't kissed them. The obvious answer is I've been grounded for the last month (it ends this weekend! Let there be light). But we're still together at school. There are so many hidden nooks and crannies around this campus. Why doesn't he pull me into one and finally seal the deal?

I know he likes me. He told me. When you like someone, you want to kiss them. Every minute we're together now, I wonder when that moment will come. It can't be any moment, it has to be THE moment. I don't want to kiss him just to get it over with, I want it to be roses and romance with unicorns frolicking around us in a lofty meadow. Maybe not that over-the-top. Omit the frolicking.

Sean's lips stop moving and his eyebrows are up in a question. I realize it's my turn to say something, but what if, instead, I just kissed him? I could lose the unicorns and dandelions. The back countertop is stacked with microscopes, and considering it all started in bio, the atmosphere is almost romantic. We can magnify our love, or something cheesy like that.

"Payton? Hello?"

I smile sweetly. "Hi."

"Don't think you can get off not listening by smiling."

"I was listening! You were saying something about that bike ride."

"It's more than just *that* bike ride. It's for a cause. For your dad. When you ride for someone, it makes it even more meaningful. And that could be the thing that pushes you to actually finish."

"I know. You're right." I lean in a bit. All I feel like doing is flirting. That's what we're supposed to do, right? Not be all serious and *connected* all the time. "Hey, do you like this shirt on me?"

"I like every shirt on you."

"Really?" I make a show of flipping my hair and I change my voice so it's more girly. "Every shirt?"

Sean laughs.

"I don't usually do purple, but I just found it in my closet—"

"You're changing the subject."

"Only because I don't want to talk about this now."

Sean rubs his temples.

"Are you getting another headache?" I ask, worried.

"I'm always getting a headache, subject changer."

"Sorry."

"Look, this is important. You know . . . I'm just glad Grady's not here."

"What does Grady have to do with a bike ride?"

"Nothing. He just thinks I'm spending too much time with you. He said—never mind."

My spine goes straight. "I'm all ears now."

"It's nothing. He just gets worried about me. Thinks you aren't into biking, that you're kind of faking it for me." Sean shakes his head. "I don't know what his deal is, he acts like there's some big secret with you."

For future reference, keep all mortal secrets from members of the underworld. Why did Jac have to tell him that stuff? Knowledge is power, and the fact that Grady knows my PFE secret has not sat well since Sean and I started hanging out. He said he wouldn't tell, but can you really take a vampire at his word?

"Whatever. He's probably spending too much time in the sun."

Sean runs his hand through his now-longer hair. "Look, the bike ride is coming up and you really need to get serious about it if you're doing it. You have to start in on sponsors and raising community awareness and—"

"You're cute when you're listing."

"This is a big deal. You know that."

"I'm in. You know I'm in. It'll be fun. I just don't like talking about it all the time. It reminds me of my dad—"

"That's a bad thing?"

"No, but I don't want to make it . . . make *him* all about his disease. And if I go around asking for sponsors, people will ask how he is and I'll have to do this brave face and . . . you might have noticed I don't do brave very well. So just sign me up and let's talk about something else."

The bell rings. Sean brushes a bang away from my face. "I'm trying to help you out here."

You ARE! Look at me. Look at you. "Yeah, well—oh!" I almost squeal, excited by the distraction. "Sub alert."

Sean turns back around and sure enough, a middle-aged balding man in a burgundy sweater vest is eyeing the class nervously. "I'm Mr. Michino. Your sub. There was an emergency and your teacher told me to ask you which videos you haven't seen."

A skater boy named Dexter in the second row raises his hand. "We've never seen the mating one. If there is a mating one. Not that we'd know, dude, because like I said, we haven't seen it."

Mr. Michino shrugs. "I get the same paycheck anyway."

"Sir?" Sean asks. I love a boy with manners.

"Yes?"

"What was the emergency?"

"Oh." Mr. Michino fakes a look of sympathy. "They were just talking about it in the teachers' lounge. Her dad died. Guess he'd had cancer for a while." He holds out his hands. "That's all I know."

Everyone murmurs, things like "I didn't even know he was sick!" "That's why she looked so beat down." "Can you imagine?" "We'll be watching videos for a month!" (Last comment from skater boy. Heart of gold, that one.) Sean keeps clenching and unclenching his jaw but says nothing. The sub turns off the lights and everyone quits talking as the snakes start getting it on.

It's fine. It doesn't affect me. It's not me—not my family. It's someone else. I don't even know her dad. It's sad, but things like that happen all the time. To other people.

But it does affect me. The fact is—that could be me. Me tomorrow, or me when I'm Miss Marietta's age. A Focus Journal or a cute boy can't protect me from something like that happening. Nothing can. The idea, the possibility, is so *real*.

A sensation grabs my chest, that feeling when your hand is asleep, except it's not my hand, it's my heart. It's not asleep, it's waking up and it aches. The sensation spreads, a tingly and excruciating numbness. Probably like the feeling my dad feels all the time.

I decide the only way to stop the numbness is to move my body. I shake my hands and pretty soon I'm shaking all over, without any extra effort. I search around the room to see if there is a corner I can hide in until I calm down.

I can't calm down.

I've been living in la-la land with Sean when people's fathers are *dying* out there. Oh my gosh, I had that entire conversation with Miss Marietta, and didn't even see what was right there. She had to live her life, come to class and teach us and the whole time she probably knew that . . . IT could happen. Any day. And it did.

I'm drowning. I hold my breath, counting the seconds until I surrender, knowing I can't come up for air. My lungs burn, my body aches, and I pray for time to stop ticking, the world to stop turning. Everything, everything just needs to stop. Now. Stop.

"Payton! Look at me!" I open my eyes and see nothing but Sean's face wrinkled in worry. "Breathe!"

I comply in a slow, exaggerated manner. Sean strokes my hand. The touch of his skin brings sensation back into my limbs. It's tingly and raw, but it's *feeling*. I can feel.

"Keep breathing."

I nod and gulp in deep breaths until I find my regular rhythm and my heart stops pounding.

His eyes are intent and it's like he felt everything I did too. "It's all right. It's all right. Everything will be fine. I promise."

I nod my head. I don't talk and neither does he. There's a little janitor in my brain, sweeping away all the unpleasant thoughts with his industrial-sized broom. It's replaced with an image of Sean's face, still gazing at me in earnest.

Sean. Sean. Sean.

Okay. I'm okay. Sean makes everything okay. Sean fills in all the cracks until I'm able to fix my attention on the video and the carefree world of mating wombats.

Everything is fine. Just breathe and watch the screen. Watch them eat, sleep, and mate. Eat, sleep, and mate.

Oh, to be a wombat.

♥ ♥ ♥

Sean was supposed to meet Grady at his mom's house after school, but he blew it off. He was supposed to study for a history quiz, but he never did. Swim season is over, but he probably would've missed that for me too.

We ditch the rest of the day and take the SEPTA bus to a cool bike shop in an old barn. We check out gears and horns and bikes and Sean tells me everything I've ever wanted to know about triathlons. He doesn't mention anyone's dad.

And I love him for it.

March 14
After Morning Bell

There is no way to organize, chart, or compartmentalize this.

    I think Sean knows.

TWENTY-THREE

PFE
Today again

Jac told him. She had to have. That's how he knows.
　He knows.

♥　♥　♥

PFE
Still now

She hates me. He hates me. She told him and now he knows about the PFEs and now I have nothing but a stupid notebook to talk to. I don't even have a counselor to read the notebook and tell me everything will be okay

or that it won't be okay or that life really
does suck or that maybe things will get better.
I don't even want it to get better because that
will give me hope, and hope . . . well, hope
sucks too.

I sound suicidal. I tear out the entry. I don't know anything for sure. Just that Sean wasn't at my locker this morning. I figured he was sick, but then I saw him in the hallway and he completely ignored me. Actually, he gave me a moody look, then ignored me. So he has to know.

It was fun while it lasted, right? Too bad he's going to hate me now. Really hate me. Maybe he'll graffiti things about me in the Hall of Terror with Grady. Maybe Jac will move in. Maybe I will really, truly have that mental breakdown I've been putting off for so long.

I freeze when I see him in bio, every muscle tensing. I'm compelled to finally slide into my seat once the bell rings, but I sit far back in my chair. If he had eyes on the back of his head, they'd be shooting me death stares.

The same sub from the previous day writes instructions on the board. Read Chapter 14 and answer study questions. I'm relieved that we have actual work today, something to keep my mind from wandering. But Sean never turns around to say hi, never even acknowledges I'm in the room. Five minutes before the bell rings, I figure I might as well face it.

"Hey," I whisper.

"Yeah?" he asks. But it isn't a question. It's a statement. A statement that is clearly stating to leave him alone.

"Um, I missed you at my locker this morning."

Sean shrugs. "Just busy. I have to finish this assignment."

Goose bumps form on my arm from his ice. When the bell rings, he gives me a little nod and leaves. Doesn't wait for me.

I should respect his space and let him talk to me when he's ready. I should. But the prospect of not talking to Sean, of losing him for even a day, is too much. I wait for him after school near the Hall of Terror. When I see him, I grab his shoulder and he stops. I don't look at him, just at my hand on his shoulder. If I'd have gone a little farther down, I could have touched his bicep. "I didn't get to see you much today."

"I know." Sean shifts his backpack to his other shoulder. "I needed some space."

"From me?"

"It's just . . . tell me about this notebook thing, Payton. Please."

Whoa. And there it is.

"I don't know what you're—"

"Don't do that. It's not fair. I've been totally honest with you. Now it's your turn."

"I have been honest with you." I drop my hand from his shoulder, my fingers warm where we touched. "I told you about the counseling sessions."

"But you didn't tell me I was a part of that somehow. That's why Ms. Callahan acted weird when she saw me, right? Am I some science experiment to you?"

"No! It's not a science experiment."

A kid bumps into me as he rushes past, hurtling me into Sean. He steadies me, but doesn't stay close. Instead, he takes a step back and folds his arms. He's doesn't look mad, exactly. Just firm. And maybe a little hurt. Which kills me.

"It's a Focus Exercise," I say.

"And that's supposed to make sense to me?"

"Ms. Callahan was trying to help me figure out things with my dad by having me focus on something else first. So I chose you. Well . . . I chose your head."

"You chose my HEAD?"

I shrink. "Uh-huh."

"So . . . you kept a whole journal about my head?"

"Yes. Well, other stuff too. But it's all nice things. You have a great head." I pause and chew my lip. "I know. I know. It's awful. I should have told you, but it's not exactly something you can slide into conversation. Besides, it gave me a chance to finally get to know you. You, and uh . . . your head."

"But I really want to make it clear here. You. Wrote. About. My. Head."

"Yes." I close my eyes and brace myself for the inevitable attack.

The onslaught of words.

The anger. The hurt. The grief.

After a few seconds of nothing, my curiosity and thirst for drama motivates me to peek out of one eye. Shockingly, Sean is grinning.

"That's the funniest thing I've ever heard! Can I read it? Where is it?"

"It's in my—wait—but I just . . . aren't you mad?"

"Sure, I *was* upset. But I thought you were using me. Were you?"

I pause. "A little, actually. At first. I was using you for therapeutic research, which is a noble thing to be used for, right?"

"A true honor."

"But it's different now. It's bigger than that."

"Bigger than my head? Is that possible?"

"I mean it. I can't explain how, but keeping this journal, it's given me something else to think about. Besides what's going on at home. And it helped me get to know you better. That's been the best part."

He laughs. "Here I'm thinking you're calling me a loser and running to your counselor for a laugh. But a—what did you call it?"

"A Focus Exercise. Well, a Focus Object."

"Oh wow, that's just brilliant."

"How did you know?" I was so careful around him. Someone had to have told him. Not Ms. Callahan—that'd break some sort of confidentiality. Grady or Jac. Jac. I still think it's Jac. She had more to gain, plus there was her iciness outside of bio. That quick run-in was probably what motivated her to tell Sean.

"Doesn't matter," he says. "What we really need to be thinking about is how I'm going to forgive you."

"Forgive me?"

"Where's this journal?"

"Sean, I would, but it's personal."

"It's my head."

"It is, but—I can't."

"Just one page. Come on."

I grudgingly take the notebook out of my backpack. What just happened? I'd worried forever he'd be so upset about it and here he is laughing at himself. I read him the first entry, the outline about his head, and he snorts so loudly at the toilet bowl line that the last few remaining students look over at us.

"What are you doing now?" Sean asks, placing his hand on my back and leading me out of the hallway. How is it every time he touches me I become so aware of that body part? It's just my back. What am I going to do when . . . if we ever kiss?

I lick my lips. Ten minutes ago I thought he would never talk to me again, and now that possibility is back out there. Seriously, he is so perfect. "Grounding doesn't end until tomorrow, but I bet my mom will let me off if I say we are doing homework. Why?"

"That's good. Go check in. Bring that notebook. First we'll burn it, then celebrate by watching the TBS *Seinfeld* marathon in my basement."

"Burn it? I don't want to burn it."

"Well, either way I'm going to buy you a new one for your next Focus Exercise."

"Which is?"

"We're going to work our way down. Next up—my neck."

♥ ♥ ♥

I change three times for our after-school hangout/book burning/date. I finally settle on my favorite pair of jeans with my red SERENITY NOW shirt. This is it. I know it. With the PFEs out in

195

the open, there's nothing between us anymore. I can almost taste his peppermint sweetness.

My top lip sweats thinking about it. I wish I knew what to expect. Where should I sit on his couch and what direction do I move my head and do we wait for a commercial break or does he really just want to watch *Seinfeld*?

I'm about to bike over to Sean's to have all these questions and more answered when he calls me. "Hey."

"Hey, I'm on my way over."

"Can we rain check it?" Sean asks.

My stomach drops. "Why?"

"I'm sorry. I've got to go back to the doctor."

"Back?"

"Yeah, I went last week because they wanted to run some tests on my headaches." He pauses. "They think they might know what's up, but they want to send me to someone else, this specialist, just to be sure. No big deal."

No Big Deal. I know very well what No Big Deal can become. "Are you going to be all right?"

"What? Oh, yeah." He voice is distant. "So we'll watch Jerry tomorrow, 'kay? I can't tell you how excited I am to hang out with you."

"Yeah, sure," I say.

"Great. Can't wait. Serenity now, right?"

"Bye, Sean."

PFE
March 14 5:23 PM

Talk about a counterproductive project.
I'm supposed to be focusing on Sean to get
over my dad's illness, only to discover Sean
is sick too. His doctor is sending him to a
specialist (ominous, right?) because he gets
headaches. So, I looked up causes of chronic
headaches and this is an annotated list of what
I found . . .

REASONS FOR HEADACHES
— Brain Tumor
— Neurological Disorders
— Migraines (can be caused by stress, which
  can be induced by a high-maintenance
  relationship, i.e., me). These also can be
  a symptom of much greater conditions.
— Other reasons that disprove my theory
  so I'm not listing them here.

Isn't it bizarre that I'm focusing on his HEAD and he gets
HEADACHES? Is this some kind of twisted joke?

This is why I never wanted to get a dog as a kid. Dogs die.
And I'm not calling Sean a dog or saying he's going to die, but
this really has just made me realize something.

Here's the thing:

By liking Sean, I'm just setting myself up for a loss. Maybe
it'll happen from a rare brain tumor. More than likely it'll be in
a few months when we decide we're over each other. Or even

more likely, he's over me. Whenever it happens, however it happens, it's going to hurt. I've seen how it works with my dad. Why am I opening myself up for it to happen again?

♥ ♥ ♥

PFE
March 14 7:12 PM

Never mind.
- Sean's the one who makes me feel secure when everything else isn't.
- He introduced me to biking. He GAVE me a bike/valentine.
- He's tried to help me work on things with my dad.
- He knows Seinfeld episode numbers!
- He's wonderful and cute and kind and perfect.

I'd be nuts to let that all go.
Nuts.

I wrap my threadbare yellow robe around me. It's past seven, and I have not heard a peep from anyone else. Normally, I would be tickled to have such privacy, but there is an eerie emptiness in the silence enveloping my home. I suddenly want to fill the void with endless chatter. To tease Trent, or maybe even tell my mom about Sean.

I slam my bedroom door shut and stomp down the stairs, waiting for someone to yell at me to cut out the noise. I want Trent or my parents to take one look at me and ask what is wrong and I want to spill it out and let the comfort roll in.

"Anyone home?" I call after all my thumping and stomping has failed to get me noticed. "Trent? Mom?"

I walk by my parents' room and hear a muffled noise coming from the master bath.

"Mom? Where is everyone?"

I poke my head into the bathroom and discover that the "noise" is my mother sobbing into one of the just-for-looks hand towels. Of course this freaks me out. Like I said, she isn't a crier. Even more frightening is the fact that my germaphobe mother is lying down with her cheek pressed to the bathroom tile. She's in her workout clothes, spandex capris and a GO GREYSTONE WILDCATS! T-shirt, headphones still in her ears. It takes her a moment to register that I'm in the room, and when she does she still doesn't move.

"Mom? What's going on? Why are you crying?"

She finally pulls herself up and leans her elbow on the toilet seat. "Come give your mommy a hug, honey."

No one, least of all my mother, has referred to her as "mommy" since I was five. I kneel down and she dwarfs me in a hug so stifling, I let out a gasp.

"Mom?" My voice is shrill. "Seriously, you're scaring me."

She jerks away from me and looks down at the tile. "This floor is disgusting. I can't remember the last time I cleaned it."

"Look at me!" I yell, and she finally looks me in the eye. She doesn't have to say anything, I already know. "It's Dad right? Is he all right?"

"He's okay . . . he's . . . This toilet seat looks diseased."

"Mom!"

"We aren't going to Florida," she says dully.

TWENTY-FOUR

The next hour is spent trying to coax my mom out of the bathroom. Once she stops crying, she insists on scrubbing the grout between the tiles, squeegeeing the shower door, and Windexing the mirror. She's about to reorganize the already alphabetized medicine cabinet when I physically force her out of the room and into her bed. She tucks the covers under her chin and lets out a deep sigh.

Her freak-out consumes me up to this point. Once she calms down, I realize I have no idea what happened to my father. It's like when you get an injury playing sports but don't realize how bad it is until after the game. The adrenaline blocks the hurt. That, or the cleaning chemicals just warped my brain. "Mom? What happened?"

She blows her nose into a soggy tissue. "Oh, honey. I'm sorry you just saw that. Your father had another episode. This time he went numb and . . . blind in his right eye."

"Blind!"

"Which is most definitely temporary, shouldn't last more

than a day or so, but it's the first time he's had this symptom and he couldn't concentrate on his patients. He sat down and when he went to stand up again he . . . couldn't. Trent left to pick him up from work and take him to the doctor since Dad obviously can't drive. Anyway, the meds he's on don't seem to be helping, so we're thinking about going to a specialist in San Francisco. And spring break won't be happening."

I exhale. I knew this would happen. I *knew* spring break wasn't going to happen. It was just a lofty daydream. Specialist. It's the second time I've heard the word today. It's so sterile and cold. And yet some random stranger would decide my family's fate. Would decide Sean's fate. "Why'd you freak me out like that? The way you were cleaning that bathroom, you'd think you were getting the house ready for his wake."

My mom shudders at the word. "Don't talk like that. Your dad will be fine. Just like before."

"Just like before . . . ," I say, but leave it at that. Nothing will ever be like it was before. We both know it.

"Hey, I'll be right back." I retrieve Dad's shirt from my room and slip it on. Mom looks at me funny when I come back.

"Isn't that your dad's shirt? He's been looking for it for weeks."

"Yeah." I crawl under the covers and snuggle next to her. "You think he'll care?"

"Are you ever going to give it back?"

"I'll buy him a new one. This one . . . I need this one for now."

Mom nods and changes the subject. "Where have you been all afternoon?"

"At home. In my room."

"I thought you were going over to Sean's house."

I swallow. "Change of plans."

"You two get in a fight?"

I shut my eyes and don't answer for a while. It's like I've experienced the three degrees of burns. Finding out about my dad's disease and lie was the first degree and it stung, finding out about Sean's headaches was the next, but now, with my dad relapsing again, I'm on my third degree, the one where the nerves are so scorched there is no sensation.

"*Mi sol*?" She strokes my hair. "Tell me what happened."

Sometimes, the only thing worse than pain is its absence. By opening up, it's like cutting myself to make sure I still bleed. So I do. I lay it all on the line. No more silent treatment. I tell her about the Focus Exercises, about the field research at the Hall of Terror. I tell her about Jac and the valentines, the real reason I wanted out of counseling. I tell her about the bike rides, the time Sean and I almost kissed, how he said he likes me and how he laughed about the PFEs. I tell her he's perfect.

I don't tell her about his headaches. Or about the struggle I just had in my journal.

My eyes are wet, and so are my mom's and we cry together, nestled under the covers, nestled there until Trent and Dad finally get home. Dad looks like a pirate with a patch over his eye and a black cane at his side. They climb into the bed to share a crowded Chinese feast.

"Hey, that's my shirt," Dad says.

"I'm borrowing it. Is that cool?"

His good eye crinkles a bit. "Maybe if you wear it, they'll actually win a game."

My dad looks the same, more tired, but you wouldn't look at him and say—That man looks sick. Except when I see my mom cut up his food for him and I think—That man, my dad, *is* sick.

No one mentions the tears, and no one mentions the spring break that never was.

♥ ♥ ♥

I wait for Sean at his locker the next morning. He looks like a mythical god today, his blond hair glowing and his smile alight. I want to kiss him so bad, but I don't. I can't. I need to be strong.

"Hey!" He leans against his locker, intoxicating me with his new bike scent. "What's up?"

"Nothing. How was the doctor?"

"They didn't detect any superpowers." He winks. "No big deal. I'm sure everything is fine. So we still doing *Seinfeld* this afternoon?"

"That's what I wanted to talk to you about." I look down at my nails. "I don't think it's a good idea."

"Don't tell me you want to watch *Friends* instead."

"No, not that." I try to look back up at Sean, but I can't quite make eye contact. I focus on his forehead instead. "I . . . actually, I don't think us hanging out . . . *period* . . . is a good idea."

Sean's smile fades. "Why?"

Why. Now there's the question. Because last night my dad came home looking like Bluebeard the pirate and I don't want to see someone I like/love hurting like that ever again. I know

204

if I said that out loud, it would sound completely crazy. I don't think it's the most sane, or even best choice I've ever made, but I thought about it all night.

It just seems stupid to open myself up to the potential for more pain. So maybe he doesn't have a brain tumor, maybe it's just headaches. If there isn't that problem, there will always be another—Jac drama or Focus Exercises or . . . anything. Anything can come between us and I can't control that. Here, now, THIS I can control.

Now my heart breaks on my own terms.

"Because, because I was using you for my Focus Exercises," I say, stumbling on the lie. "That's what this was all about. That's why we were even . . . friends. So I think it's best, you know, if we both just kind of move on."

"If this is about your focus things, I already told you I'm over it."

"Yeah, well, I'm not."

"You're not," he says.

"No." I raise my chin. "I can't write about you anymore, and that's why we were hanging out anyway."

"All right." Sean runs his hand through his hair. "All right. Is this about something else? I'm really confused."

"No. It's just . . . you're just going to get in the way of what I need to do. I need to be alone."

Sean takes a step closer to me and lowers his voice. "Look, if you need space, I can give you space. Call me the space man. I know things are tough but—"

I don't deserve him. I don't deserve the worried look he's giving me. I really wish he would stop being so wonderful.

"Yes. Space." I try to make my voice flat. "For good though. Forever. Nothing personal."

"Nothing personal, huh?" Sean asks, his voice catching.

"I'm sorry, but . . . I'm sorry. That's how I feel."

I'm reminded of the movies where the main character takes in a wild animal and for whatever reason, has to let it go. They go out to some field, usually at sunset to serve some metaphorical purpose, and lets the animal loose before turning away. The animal doesn't budge so the person starts yelling at the animal, "Go on, boy. Get out of here. We don't want you!" And the animal doesn't understand, thinks it really isn't wanted when really, *really* that couldn't be any further from the truth.

Sean looks away from me. "I think I know why you like *Seinfeld* so much. You're just like Jerry. You have something good with someone and let the tiniest flaw ruin that. I don't know what checks I have against me, what you see wrong with me, but just so you know, everyone has flaws." He shakes his head, and I die a little inside when he turns away from me. He pauses before looking back and saying, "Everyone, Payton. Even you."

It's the truest thing he's ever said. Except, he's not flawed—he's so perfect that he manages to end an argument, end a relationship, with a dead-on *Seinfeld* reference. I watch him walk away and lean my head against my locker.

And just like I knew it would, I can feel my heart break again.

TWENTY-FIVE

<u>PFE</u>
March 15: 4:41 PM
Topic: The quest for a new Focus Object

- My bedroom ceiling has that popcorn covering
  on it that causes asbestos or something but at
  least hides a bad paint job.
- I wonder if the builders knew how many
  hours I would spend admiring their ceiling
  handiwork, creating shapes and images from
  the swirly designs in the ceiling?
- There's a vampire right above my bed, a
  bicycle in the far left corner, and I swear
  the water stain next to the closet is an
  exact replica of Sean's head.
- Bet that's loaded with hidden meanings.
  Ms. Callahan would have a field day if she

ever read this thing. Maybe her insights would actually help.

- *Great, now I'm missing Ms. Callahan. Solitary confinement really does cause insanity.*

♥ ♥ ♥

Breaking up with Sean (well, we weren't together. Cut things off? Unfriended?) makes me realize just how much I hate to be alone. I cry a lot when there is no one to witness it. Being alone makes me think about things . . . about Sean, which is a topic I need to UN-focus on from now on.

Un-focusing, as it turns out, is harder than focusing. I can't just turn off my brain or my heart. I may have pushed him away physically, but the boy is still haunting me.

So I double my spin class sign-ups. Spin is the best brain emptier. Luckily, I discovered that Trent has a secret crush on Yessica and use this information to con him into driving me to the Y in exchange for an introduction. He makes me practice the conversation we'll have, the conversation that begins, "Oh, there you are, little sis. I was just helping out a senior citizen in need at the pool. And who is your friend—"

Trent's got the punk rock at full ear-destruction mode. He stops at a red light and uses his free hands to wow me with his air guitar skills. I look past him at the shopping complex right next to the gym and see a florist. It reminds me of our biology lesson on pollination, which makes me think of Miss Marietta and boom—an idea. A fuzzy idea, but it seems important for some reason.

"Hey, can we stop at that flower shop real quick? It will only take a second."

"Sending tulips to your boyfriend? Let me guess the card— 'Our tulips should be one lip.'"

"He's not my boyfriend," I snap. "And even if he was, things are over now, so stick to your stupid air guitaring and shut up."

The light turns green and without saying a word Trent turns left into the shopping center. He parks in front of the florist, turns down the music, and says softly, "Take as long as you need."

It's 5:50 and the sign on the door says they close at 6:00. No one is behind the counter, so I clang the bell.

"Hello? I know you're about to close but I need—"

A woman so small and skinny she could be Tinker Bell's body double appears from the back room, dressed in a prim periwinkle suit, a tulip pinned in the lapel. She looks like she should be at afternoon tea, not selling carnations in a strip mall. When she speaks, it's with a British accent.

"What can I get you?"

"Flowers."

"I think we have a few of those lying around."

I close my eyes and form my words carefully. I hadn't realized why exactly I was here until this point.

"My teacher's dad died."

The woman, Fern according to her name tag—although that is too cute of a coincidence to be real—clucks her tongue. "Are you looking into a burial wreath?"

"You mean those things with carnations? Heck no." I scrunch up my nose. "I want something for her. Is that weird? I didn't know her dad, and I've never done this. I mean, never bought flowers for . . . a situation like this."

"There are plenty of flower rules. What color and when to send and what size. But the best rule to follow is your instincts. If you want something to comfort her, think of who she is as a person and what kind of flower would give her happiness or peace."

Miss Marietta as a person? I know maybe three things about her. She likes, or maybe liked, to party. She likes science. Her dad is dead. What flower sums it all up? Exotic flowers seem too wild for her, but traditional roses are too tame. And who came up with condolence flowers anyway? They're a slap in the face. Flowers die. Why give the mourner more to mourn about?

I look around the shop, my attention diverted by a large banana plant in the corner. It reminds me of Miss Marietta's lectures, how her eyes sparkled when she shared the joys of pollination. "We can learn a lot from the plant world," she'd said. "Survival seems unlikely. The fate of you and your posterity are usually beyond your control. A strong wind. Forgiving soil. A hungry insect. But there's a certain amount of grace, giving yourself up to the hope that things will work out if you, the plant, just produce as many seeds as possible. With enough work, enough effort, one of those seeds will grow."

"This is going to sound weird, but do you send just regular plants?" I ask. "It seems kind of sad to send something that will die when someone . . . isn't here anymore. I want to give her something alive."

"She'd have to take care of it."

"Yeah. I think that's the point."

"I have just the thing." Fern plops a large, worn catalog onto the counter and flips to the back. "There. How's this?"

She points to an exotic-looking tree with sharp crimson flowers and palm tree–like bark. The name has one too many syllables for me to pronounce. Three feet tall, according to the catalog description, and first found on a Polynesian island. Folklore says the blossoms are reincarnated souls looking for peace. "Perfect. Is it expensive?"

"It's not a handful of dandelions. But, like you said, it's perfect."

"I'll need a card too. And I want to write it myself."

She leads me over to a rack of cards. I pick one out, wispy clouds with "Deepest Sympathies" on the front, and stare at the vast, white blankness inside. I'm supposed to fill it with words of solace. Somehow, "Sorry about your dad" doesn't seem right. Maybe I should color the whole inside of the card black, because that's how I felt when I found out about my dad, and that's how I'd feel if he ... was in the same situation as Miss Marietta's dad.

"When do you want this delivered?" Fern asks.

I have no idea where Miss Marietta lives. Until recently, she was my lush partying bio teacher, not a person with a home and a father. My bright idea is dimming with each step. "You know, I don't even know where it's going exactly."

"It's a special order, so it won't be ready until Thursday. Why don't you call me and let me know what you want to do then. And that'll give you time to work on the card."

The store door chimes tinkle as Trent huffs in. "Can you

hurry? You don't want to be late for your class. *I* don't want you to be late for your class."

I hold out my hand. "Give me some money."

"Whatever, beggar. I'm broke."

"Yeah right. We both know you make crazy money."

"It's all in savings."

"Then give me Dad's just-for-emergencies credit card."

"You're going to use Dad's own credit card to buy him flowers?"

I scoff. "I'm not buying flowers for Dad."

"I thought you said you and that boy were off."

I pat my open palm. "They're for my teacher."

"Look, sis." Trent shifts uncomfortably. "I saw this episode on *Dateline* and guys can get in some serious trouble—"

"My *female* teacher whose dad just died. Do I need to deliver his eulogy to you or will you give me the money?"

He grumbles but hands me the credit card. "You better pay Dad back."

"I will. Just as soon as I get a job."

He swears under his breath and walks back to the car. Five minutes later I join him, still-blank card in hand, wondering what I could write that would possibly do Miss Marietta any good.

♥ ♥ ♥

Yessica is in a particularly heinous—or maybe it's good— mood that evening. It's hard to tell because no matter the range of her emotions, she kicks our butts. Tonight, I'm faking the ride, too busy thinking about everything else to care about my intensity level. Around me, the other riders are in a similar mode, going through the motions and praying Yessica won't single them out. Halfway through the ride, Yessica senses the class apathy and turns off the music.

"All right. We're going to take a break. Story time. Go ahead and cruise, you'll know when it's time to go again."

Too tired to care, we comply.

"I want you to imagine you're in the African wilderness. That's right, an African wilderness. Straight-up *Lion King* here, folks. You're walking down a trail, no, *crawling* down a trail because you're so thirsty. Put that water down, Frank."

Frank ducks his head and sticks his bottle back in place.

"So. You're thirsty. You see an oasis in the distance, and you know the only way you're going to survive is if you get to it. Okay, start pedaling. Don't go nuts, resistance is low, let's just get it going."

We pedal, glances passed among strangers. A safari in the middle of spin class. Now it's happened. Yessica has lost it.

"You're almost out of energy, so it's going to take everything you have in your core to make it. You're focused on that oasis. You're not worrying about how you look in your safari wear or how much it hurts to keep going. All that matters is the water."

I'm getting into it now, less aware of what the other spinners are doing. I like the whole not-thinking thing. Jungles, oasis, whatever . . . just keep me going.

"Now, Africa isn't the most forgiving place, and as luck

213

would have it, a big old jaguar is behind you now on the path, eyeing your butt as you pump on that bike."

I look back at my butt. I could feed the whole jungle.

Yessica flips the music back on. "Welcome to the Jungle" by Guns and Roses blares from the speakers. "Now get going! There is water at the oasis. Water and fat antelope that will make that jaguar forget about your scrawny butt. You're biking toward something and away from something but it's the same direction. The same goal. Now, straight sprint until the end of the song. GO! GO! GO!"

Faster and faster my legs turn, except I'm not thinking about the ride or the pain. It's something Yessica said. Biking toward something and away from something and it's the same place. I should be getting something out of it, I know it, but I can't quite grasp how it applies to me. I wish I had someone to explain it better.

The song ends and we all grab our water bottles. Yessica begins the toweling off ritual. You know, I bet Yessica and Ms. Callahan would be great friends. They could sit around and spit self-help garbage out to each other. And they're both big on the focusing thing. Except Yessica's a little more one-dimensional. Her solution to everything is to spin harder. Ms. Callahan, if I were still seeing her, would slow the wheels down. Maybe Ms. Callahan is like the water or jaguar or something. Whatever— the metaphor is played out.

But you know what? Maybe it's not a bad idea for me to take the help that is available, to not be the idiot who won't drink the water being handed to them. I should probably go suck up to Ms. Callahan and see what advice she has about all this crap I have going on now. At least her form of therapy is a lot more forgiving to my butt.

♥ ♥ ♥

I'm sitting outside Ms. Callahan's office the next morning before she's even there. There's that bad coffee and paper smell that dominates school offices. The secretary keeps glancing at me, then the clock, then the counselor's door. Finally she asks, "What time was your appointment, dear?"

"Oh, I don't really have one. I just need to talk."

"Ms. Callahan is always the last one here." She cocks her head to the side. "You might want to get to class."

I grip the sides of the brown upholstered chair, prepared to stage a sit-in if I have to. "It's kind of an emergency."

"Do you want me to have someone come and get you out of class?"

"I want to sit right here in this chair until my guidance counselor walks through that door."

The secretary shrugs and turns on her radio station again. Michael Bolton this time. Save me, Ms. Callahan.

Three minutes before the morning bell, Ms. Callahan breezes in wearing what can only be described as a muumuu. I don't know if I've ever seen a muumuu before, but I'm pretty sure this fits the description. Big, shapeless dress in a print screaming, "Hey, is the *dress* big and shapeless or is it just *me*?"

Ms. Callahan is halfway to her office before she even notices I'm there. "We don't have an appointment, do we?"

"No, but . . . do you have a minute?"

"I have three," she says with the slightest edge in her voice.

"I'll take it." I follow her into her office, where she heaves a large grocery bag onto her desk. A few cans of cat chow, the gourmet kind, roll onto the floor.

"Oh, Mr. Nippers won't be happy!" She sighs.

"Who?"

"Mr. Nippers. My cat. He hates dented cans."

Mr. Nippers. Riiiiight. She sweeps the cans back into the bag, plops into her swivel chair, and looks up at the ceiling. "All right, Payton. What can I do for you?"

"Okay. Look. I never gave you a fair shot. I never gave any of this a fair shot. I'm sorry for that, and I'm sorry for the fight with Jac. I'm all alone now and I could really use some help."

Ms. Callahan busies herself shuffling papers around her desk. She's looking down and she starts sniffing. Crap. Please don't start crying. I do not need to deal with another emotional person. I'm emotioned out.

She nods toward the seat in front of her desk and I take it. She clears her throat a few nasty phlegmy times before looking me square in the eye and saying, "Let's figure this out."

TWENTY-SIX

It's pretty easy to like Ms. Callahan once I decide I don't hate her. That, and it's kind of hard to dislike someone when all they do is sit there and listen to me lament about life's perils for sixty minutes, even when she said she only had three and even though she gets five calls on the intercom while I'm talking. And when I'm telling her everything, she never says, "Start talking to your dad or open yourself up to Sean." Not all problems are that cut and dry. Mine's more cut, wash, rinse, repeat.

When I'm done, she gently recommends self-explorATION as a cure for my alienATION, which is personally one too many *-ations* for me, but I let it go.

"But don't you think I've done enough self-exploration? Can't I do some team searching or something?"

"With whom? You've severed ties with those you love."

"Well, what if I fix that?"

"Is that what you want?" she asks.

"I don't want to make things better. I just want them to *be* better. I want the problems that caused all my messed-up relationships to just be gone so everything can be right again."

"Well, sorry, but that's not going to happen. Think about it for a moment. I'm going to get some coffee." She leaves and returns with two mugs. She passes me mine—purple with cartoon hands clasped and printed with the prayer, "Lord, please help me accept what I can't change and change what I can't accept."

I set it down on her desk without taking a sip.

"Start small," she says. "What do you think is the easiest fix?"

"Well, making up with Jac maybe, although I wouldn't call it easy . . ."

"But easiest."

"Probably. Yeah."

"Try talking to her. See where it goes. Things can't get any worse than how they are, right?"

I nod noncommittally. If there is one thing I've learned in the last few months, things can *always* get worse.

♥ ♥ ♥

I think about it for two days and finally decide to just do it. Talk to Jac again. So maybe she hates me, maybe I'll confirm my suspicion that she blabbed to Sean and then hate her, but at least we're moving in a new direction. I'm being proactive. Or something.

I already know one thing that'll help, and I hide it in my locker the next day. Unfortunately for me, I have no idea where Jac is. Now that we've switched our hallway routes, I don't know which way she gets to class. I try to hang by her locker, but this short Hispanic kid comes up and opens it. I start to ask why he is breaking into my friend's locker when I see a bunch of anime pictures hanging inside. Jac locker swapped.

Bio is shot because we're in the small theater listening to a guest lecture by some nuclear physicist who discovered a rare bug (or maybe a sickness? A virus? A computer virus? Obviously I'm alert). Can't be that important of a scientist if a high school is on her lecture circuit.

I'm yanked from my vegetative state when I overhear the skater kid, Dexter, talking to one of his shaggy-haired buddies about prank ideas. At first, it's annoying chatter, but then I think of an idea of how I can use the Dextmeister to my advantage.

"You guys want pranks?" I lean in between them. We're in the farthest backseats of the theater, close to the door where I hoped to corner Jac after the bell.

"You think you can pull a prank?"

"No. I think you can."

Dexter shrugs. "What is it?"

"Fire alarm."

His buddy snickers. "That's original. Maybe we'll put a tack on teacher's chair too."

"Yeah, or stick ABC gum in her hair."

I lean back, my hands behind my head. "Suit yourselves. I mean, we do have the most anal hall monitors ever, and the alarms are now encased in glass and displayed in highly visible areas. You'd have to be Tom Cruise in *Mission: Impossible* to make it happen, which is why we've never had a bogus fire drill, like, *ever*. But, you're right. It's elementary school stuff. Stick to Ex-lax in the brownies. Or whatever you guys put in there."

Dexter eyes me suspiciously. "How do you know all that?"

"You're looking at the leader of the school safety council two semesters running."

"Impressive." They giggle. Like little girls. Doubt they do that around their skating friends. They'd be kicked off the half pipe. Whatever that is.

"Fine. I'm just the only one who knows the hall monitors' schedules and where the cameras are and which alarm to pull. But if you're not interested—"

"What's in it for you?" Dexter asks.

"Um . . ." I blink a few times. "Pure fun?"

They stare at me expectantly.

"Look, I could use a little rule-breaking in my life. Just do it and I swear upon my brother's life I won't tell a soul."

The boys study each other for a moment.

"Dude, should we?" Dexter asks.

"It'd be killer."

"We would reign."

"So, it's on?" I interrupt before they grow some brain cells and realize the likelihood of a girl like me blindly aiding their master plans is slim to zilch.

They do that thing with their fingers that Trent always does when he's head banging. I think it means love or maybe it's the devil. Either way they are grinning.

"Prank or die."

♥ ♥ ♥

The guys pull it off without a hitch during fifth period. Well, there was the hitch where they got caught, but that wasn't on me. I told them the perfect setup, but after Dexter rang the bell his friend called him a glory hog and they started to brawl. The hall monitor found them right as the fire truck arrived, and both guys kept fighting over who pulled the alarm.

My plan: during my time on the school safety committee, I'd designed a seamless exit route for the entire school. I'd also figured out how to have Jac and me close together no matter what period it happened. We had a safety spot on every side of the school.

When the alarm goes off, I rush to my locker, grab Jac's surprise, and hurry to our spot. I stand under the large dogwood tree adjacent to the portables, which is on a hill so I can overlook the chaos and devastation should a true disaster occur.

The only glitch is Jac and the question—will she show? I watch as the entire school pours out of the doors, laughing and gossiping, unaware of the petrified girl under the tree. I search in vain for Jac's golden hair, and when the principal blows the horn signaling it's time to get back to class, I almost kneel down and cry.

"It was an inferno in there," someone says behind me.

"That's the coward that left us to die." I answer automatically and turn around to see Jac. It's our safety phrase, derived from the *Seinfeld* when George pushes the women, children, and clown out of the way at a birthday party to escape the threat of fire. He's yelling at an EMT and the whole crowd comes up to confront him. Maybe you had to be there. But regardless, it is the phrase I made Jac memorize when devising our safety route. She'd argued we could just look at each other to see if we were okay, but the quote tests the mental capabilities and—

"Have I ever told you how stupid that safety phrase is?" Jac plops down onto the ground and twists off a piece of grass.

"I told you. Physical confirmation of our well-being isn't enough. We need . . ." I trail off, realizing we are now talking, an event that has not happened in over a month. I ease down next to her on the grass and watch as the last of the students disappear into the school.

"I'm surprised you haven't let Sean in on the code," she says with a flip of her hair. "Isn't *Seinfeld* part of your love language or something?"

"Please don't talk about Sean," I say.

"Why not?"

"We aren't talking."

Her eyes widen. "You aren't talking? I thought you were sitting in a tree, K-I-S-S-I—"

"No. And I can't talk to you about it right now."

"Would you get over that stupid valentine already? It got you the boy, right? Move on."

The anger is bubbling up again and I keep it down by focusing on the tree trunk, dissecting the nicks in the bark, searching for a Virgin Mary or Sean's head, but all I see are expressionless lines. Someone carved X.T. AND H.B. forever in the bark, then crossed it out and wrote "Xavier is a tool." H.B. has moved on, and I want to do the same. "I'm not talking about the valentine. You clued him in on the PFEs. Why'd you do that, Jac? Sure, we're in a fight and it's THE fight, the one that busts up friendships. We said awful things and you totally hate me now. Fine. But couldn't you have just hated me in silence? Did you have to ruin our friendship *and* my relationship with Sean?"

The focus on the tree has given me the strength to lay it on the line, and the last shot of adrenaline gives me the courage to look at Jac. I flinch. Her eyes are bright with fire.

"I can't believe you," she says softly.

"Me? You can't believe ME?"

The fire in her eyes is suddenly extinguished by her tears. "I can't believe that you for one second would believe I would *ever* tell Sean about your journal! All I've done is try to help you with him. I mean, except for during that cell quiz thing, but even then he was all about you."

"Jac, I saw how you looked at me when we ran into each other in front of biology class. Like you seriously wanted to destroy me. You hate me now, admit it."

"I don't hate you!"

"You could have fooled me."

"No. First off, you haven't exactly been sending warm fuzzies my way either."

"Well, sorry if I haven't been feeling warm and fuzzy—"

"Stop. My turn. You know, you can be so self-centered. Maybe it's not all about you. Maybe I'm dealing with this too. All of it. Maybe I'm mad at myself for not seeing what you needed. I'm not like you. I don't make spreadsheets on my friend's steps for self-improvement."

"It wasn't a spreadsheet," I argue. But she's right. We aren't alike, at least not in that sense. But it's always worked for us before.

She yanks some more grass. "Well, I'm a horrible friend. Sorry I don't know my computer programs."

"I didn't come here to fight," I say. "Let's not waste my carefully orchestrated fire alarm."

"Oh, like Ms. Safety Committee had anything to do with the fire alarm."

A smile spreads across my face. "Wanna bet?"

"You didn't."

"Well, Skater Dexter was in on the plan. I've been trying to find a way to talk to you and . . . this was it. I had to get you to talk to me."

Jac jumps up and does a dance right there under the tree, the beads in her braids clinking together. She's laughing so hard that the gyrations are spastic, a thrust here, then a giggle. And she's crying. I watch in awe.

"You wild child! A fire alarm. I love it! That is the sweetest thing anyone has ever done! A whole school outside in my honor. I can't believe you'd risk that for me. No one I . . . no one in my life has ever . . . Thank you." She stops dancing for an instant. "You're my best friend. And I didn't tell, Payton. Swear it."

I switch from seething mad to pure elation in five seconds flat. I hadn't thought of the fire alarm as a gift, but I'm not about to take it away. She doesn't get many presents that aren't picked out by her dad's girlfriend.

Jac's enthusiasm is pure electricity. My body jolts up in response and I dance. Even if we're in full view of nearby traffic. Even if I'm supposed to be in class. Because she didn't tell! And I'm dancing with my best friend.

I remember the therapy right in the middle of the moon-walk. "Wait! We have to end the fight. I brought something for you. To show I'm sorry for being such a massive jerk."

I retrieve the plastic bag I hid on the other side of the dogwood and dump the contents onto the grass. "*Hoppy* Easter!"

Candy-filled Easter eggs spill onto the grass. Jac picks one up and shakes it.

"I kind of bombed Valentine's," I say. "And you've tried to help me, really. I'm not going to lie—your uh . . . level of involvement did freak me out, but that's how you are and I love it about you. Usually."

"And usually it's okay, but I probably did go too far. I do that sometimes."

"Wait, let me tell you about the present. So since I bombed Valentine's and Easter is coming up, I thought we could have an egg hunt. Just, you know, for fun."

She cracks open an egg and chews a jellybean. "It's perfect."

"It's nothing," I say.

She seizes me in a giant squeeze. "I really am sorry I pushed you into Sean. I'm sorry about all my pushing," she whispers, suddenly serious.

"I probably never would have talked to him if you hadn't."

"But I know how you are and should have gone at Payton pace, not Jac speed."

"It's fine," I say.

"He's a great guy."

"Yeah, well, I let him go."

"What do you mean?" she asks.

"I . . . I don't know. I had to do it, and now it's like . . . it's like I'm broken. I miss him so much."

"It'll work out. You deserve each other. You deserve the best."

I close my eyes and squeeze her harder. "*We* deserve each other."

She squeezes me until I can't breathe. "How much longer are we going to hug like this?"

We let go and laugh, then squeal and hug each other again.

♥ ♥ ♥

PFE
March 19 9:32 PM

I'm not going to spend a bunch of time dwelling on this because the damage is done, the water is under the bridge, the road has been crossed, the song has been sung, BUT—Jac did not tell Sean. And unless Ms. Callahan is the world's worst counselor ever, she didn't either. There is one other person who knew about the PFE. I would kill him for disclosing my secret, but he is already kind of sort of dead.

For Grady's sake, I hope Ms. Callahan does a session on Anger Management issues <u>real</u> soon.

TWENTY-SEVEN

<u>PFE</u>
March 20 10:54 AM

Have you ever lost a pair of jeans and thought they were gone forever and you bought other jeans that look good in their own way and made you happy but nothing fit you like THOSE jeans, but then you find those jeans and you realize your butt looks even better in them than you remembered, as if your butt was made for the jeans and the jeans were made for your butt?

Jac and I are back. I don't know who is the butt and who is the jeans.

Metaphors definitely aren't my thing.

♥ ♥ ♥

Jac and I go right back to our old life the next day. The life where we meet in between classes, walk home, e-mail, and talk on the phone. Our life before Sean.

Although, we can never totally go back to how things were because I am still keenly aware of his existence. Every time I see his big old head bobbing across the quad, I feel like a phoenix—bursting into flames only to cool off before rising up and doing it all over again. But I did it to myself. It's a choice I have to deal with. It's this choice that a small part of me deep, deep inside thinks might have been wrong. Because either way, I'm not happy without him. He was my daily fix. Now there's just another hole I have to figure out how to fill.

So, with the aid of Jac, I go into full 007 mode with the Great Plant Idea. We find Miss Marietta's home address online, which is only a quarter of a mile away from me. Jac insists on writing the card, which works for me since my dreams lately have been haunted by its endless blankness. My job is to pick up the plant, which I do with the help of a begrudging Trent. Jac meets me at the front of our teacher's housing community at 1500 hours.

"Do you have the card?" I peek out from behind one of the plant's massive spikes.

"You didn't ask that right. Code, remember?"

I roll my eyes. "Has the white dove landed?"

"Roger. Are you ready to deliver the green goblin?" Green goblin = well, duh, right? Our code talk is more obvious than Pig Latin.

After a secret handshake and three strolls around the block to "stake out the place"—in case, you know, Russian spies try to thwart the delivery—we ease the plant onto the doorstep.

Jac places a gloved finger over her lips while she rings the doorbell. Then we sprint to the hedge lining the right side of her yard. We should just run away altogether to avoid getting caught. It works better if Miss Marietta doesn't know who the plant is from. The anonymity, the awareness that it could be anyone in the universe—or at least our high school—thinking of her is what she needs. When she comes back to school, she'll look at each student and wonder, and the mystery will shift the focus. It will ease the pain. At least, that's how it would work for me if I were in her shoes.

I hope I'm never in her shoes.

She opens the door. She's in a fuzzy orange robe, her hair pulled back in a tight ponytail. Even from across the yard between tree branches, the grief is etched on her face. She plucks the card out of the plant, which is complete dessert for us. I thought she'd just take the plant in. This way we get to see her read the card.

When she first starts reading, she keeps looking at the plant, like she's trying to connect what the card says with this massive creature invading her doorstep. But halfway through her face relaxes. Her eyes dart across her yard, but never settle on one thing long enough for her to see us behind the hedge. Then she picks up the plant, gingerly touching the spikes, and the last thing we see before she closes the door is the faintest suggestion of a smile.

"That was amazing." I breathe out. "What did you write?"

I glance over at Jac and see her face is streaked in tears. "That stuff you said about plant cells," she says.

"No one reacts like that to plant cells. Not even Miss Marietta."

Jac lies down on the grass, her arms crossed over her body like a corpse. The tears are still falling, down the corner of her eye and into her hair. "I added a little bit more."

"Like . . ."

"I just said I know what it's like to lose your dad."

You know in those old cartoons how there's always an Acme anvil hitting the characters when they finally realize something? I felt like a whole factory full of those things were knocking me out. Of course she knew what it was like. Jac hadn't always been Jac, the girl with the divorced parents who gets to do whatever she wants. She used to have a dad and a mom who, okay, fought a lot, but there was some sort of unit there. Having a dad gone because he can't help it is one thing. Having a dad leave by choice is another.

"You do know how it feels, don't you?"

She hiccups. "Yeah."

"I'm sorry."

"You helped me out when he left," she says. "It feels good to be able to help her."

We both don't say anything, thinking the same thing. I say it first. "My dad isn't gone."

"Nope."

"I should stop acting like he is."

"Uh-huh."

"I don't know how to do that."

"Yes you do."

And suddenly I'm overwhelmed by another feeling, but this one lifts me up instead of weighing me down.

This gazillion-kilowatt lightbulb is just glowing over my head. I now have a new force to focus all my energy on, now that that other focus thing we don't need to mention is un-focusable.

I'm doing it. The MS 150, a bike ride to help fund MS research. Have I mentioned my dad has multiple sclerosis, a crippling disease that affects hundreds of thousands of Americans every year? There isn't a cure—yet. (I got that blurb from the brochure. I find the yet part to be particularly motivating. See? I'm totally serious. Signed up and read an official brochure.)

So, it's all come full circle. Ms. Callahan had me think about other things so I might eventually get to my dad's MS, and I'd say a bike ride in his honor is pretty dang close.

Jac's helping me look for sponsors. That girl should really look into something like event planning or car sales. Maybe Sean's mom can get her into realty.

Uh, I hate when he pops up like that. Like the cork on the champagne. Right in my eye.

TWENTY-EIGHT

The weather warms enough for me to bike outside again, and I'm at Valley Forge every afternoon. Although I feel him in every loop and curve I ride, I don't physically see Sean once. He's probably found a new route. Which makes me glad, obviously, because it sucks seeing him. But also . . . well, it sucks *not* seeing him.

I go to my dad's office, my mom's book club, the Y, my school office, a practice for my old basketball team, anyplace where the name Payton Gritas might be familiar so I can raise more money. Each cent donated gives me more accountability to finish the ride and makes me less likely to quit when I'm alone on that bike with nothing but the thought of why I'm there to begin with to keep me going.

My mom and dad leave for San Francisco the Friday before spring break so they can see the Specialist, the mighty man who will hopefully wave his I-have-a-bazillion-dollar-degree wand and make some magic happen. Dad finally got to take the patch off, though the vision in his right eye isn't fully restored.

He still has the cane—he doesn't use it all the time, but it's gut wrenching to watch him when he does. Yet, even as I watch him hobble into his car, there's a tiny feeling nibbling inside me. Despite everything I've seen him go through, I still need to believe that he can get better. I still hope.

The last day of school is filled with word searches and videos and other teacher time wasters. I get called down to the office during final period. Ms. Callahan is standing behind her desk when I get there. A blue striped bag, decorated with a not-so-cute cartoonish duck, sits expectantly in front of her. She claps when she sees me and motions toward the gift.

"I just wanted to give you a little present before your big race," she says with a benevolent smile.

"Uh, thanks!" Please don't let it be a muumuu. I pull each sheet of green tissue paper out of the bag and fold it neatly next to the gift. When there's nothing between me and Ms. C's token of thoughtfulness, I close my eyes and reach inside. My hand closes around something furry and I open my eyes to see what looks like a dead rodent. I drop it on the desk fast.

"What is it?!"

Ms. Callahan scoops up the fur ball and holds it up to the sunlight leaking through her blinds. "This is Fuzzy."

"I can see that it's fuzzy. Does it have rabies too?"

She laughs and tosses it to me. "It's not alive, Payton."

It's not. It's a toy mouse, the kind filled with catnip that has a little bell jingling inside. The fur is matted, and one of the button eyes is missing. She's given me a used cat toy. I'm taking counseling sessions from a woman who thinks this . . . this thing is an appropriate gift idea.

"A mouse. I'm lost."

"It belongs to Mr. Nippers. Well, belonged. Now it's yours. I bought him a new Focus Object."

"This? So . . . your CAT has a Focus Object?"

"I'm a big fan of them, if you can't tell. Mr. Nippers was mine after my divorce."

"Divorce?" I ask in a croaky gasp.

"You're looking at the former Mrs. Otis Bartisqua. You can see why I went back to the maiden name."

"Sure. But . . . wait. So you're giving me your Focus Object's Focus Object? I'm totally lost."

Ms. Callahan motions for me to take a seat. "Otis and I were best friends as kids, high school sweethearts, got married in college. He knew me inside and out. And then he didn't. Somewhere along the line, we both let it go. I didn't realize how much until he served me with divorce papers. So there I am, thirty-eight and without my Otis for the first time in my life. I took to watching quite a bit of Food Network, and was on my way to buy one of those sharp Japanese knives I saw on a commercial when I saw Mr. Nippers in a pet shop window."

She strokes the nearest picture of her beloved feline. "He was playing with that cat toy with such concentration, such focus. It's what I remembered my life being, all in a direct line, all working for a goal, before Otis left. So I bought him. Took him home. Ditched the Food Network addiction and gave everything I had to Mr. Nippers. He became my Focus Object.

"I would watch him for hours playing with that toy, swatting at it, hunting it. He never seemed to care that he couldn't ever conquer it. It was the pursuit, the promise that kept him going.

And by shifting all my energy onto Mr. Nippers, it gave me time to heal the Otis wound. We're friends now. And I've involved myself in more things. But I still have Mr. Nippers. It wasn't one or the other. I got both."

"But I'm not over my dad and I don't have Sean—my Focus Object."

"While I do believe your apparent choice in a Focus Object was . . . unconventional, to say the least, I still think he might have helped. Mr. Nippers didn't make everything with Otis go away. That's not the point of a Focus Object. If it was, you wouldn't be any different than a cutter or a bulimic, transferring your pain into something else. It's not a permanent fix. But sometimes, Payton, you have to take the scenic route, even when there is a straight road ahead of you."

I jingle the mouse in the palm of my hand. One eyeball seems to wink at me. Mr. Nippers will find a new Focus Object. This race is mine. The fact that I might run into the former object of my affection, well . . . I'll deal with that when I have to.

♥ ♥ ♥

Mom and Dad are set to call that night and give us the word from the almighty Specialist. The thing with MS is, there is no Plan A or Plan B. What applies today might not tomorrow. They might say my dad is all right, to stick with his meds, or maybe switch his meds and the flare-up should resolve itself. Or that he's gone to the next level, that he will continue to deteriorate, that sensation will never return. And they might give him a big "Heck if we know" and send him along his uncertain way.

Trent has finally faced his fears and asked Yessica out, and true to her name, she complied. He's sitting at the kitchen counter, tapping his nails on the granite. They're well-groomed, along with the rest of him—hair slicked back but not greasy, button-down blue shirt and designer jeans. His nervous energy shifts from staring at the phone to staring at the clock. Mom and Dad still haven't called and it's already seven. He's set to pick up his workout goddess in thirty minutes. I plop down next to him and join in the fidgeting. Trent was supposed to drop me off at Jac's a half an hour ago so we could go to the pre–bike ride bash put on for all the volunteers and cyclists. I don't mention to Trent that we're late. The phone call takes precedence.

After hours, or minutes or seconds—time is lost at this point—the phone rings. We stare at each other, frozen, until Trent snaps out of it and grabs the phone on the third ring.

"Dad? Oh." He hands me the phone wordlessly.

"Hello?"

"Payt? I tried your cell. What's going on?"

"Jac. We're waiting to hear from my dad. Do you want to just go and I'll meet you there?"

"Roger."

"Who's Roger?" I ask.

"It means ten-four."

"Huh?"

"You are so not James Bond. Have Trent drop you off at the party. I'll see you there."

I hang up and look again at the clock. A quarter to. Trent is going to be late. "Jac's going to meet me at the party, so you can just drop me off there. Whenever we go."

Trent looks at the clock too and shakes his head. "I'm going to have to go now."

"What?"

"Hey, whether it's me or you picking up the phone, it doesn't matter. I'm going to go get Yessica, we'll come get you, and then we'll drop you off at your thing."

"You're leaving me here alone?" My palms begin to itch and I alternate scratching each hand. "Can't Mom call your cell or something? I mean, you're the one who knows what's going on; if they tell me news, it might not even make sense. Don't you think—"

"I'm going to get Yessica. You're the one that wanted to be included on all the family stuff, remember? The phone can't bite."

Yes it can. At least, the info relayed by the phone can. Twelve minutes later it rings again. Each ring is like the hiss of a rattlesnake, warning me not to come any closer. But thanks to Trent's sudden absence, I have no choice.

"Hello?" I say in the faintest whisper of a voice.

"Payton?" It's Caleb. He sounds far away. Probably because he is. "Hey, is Trent around?"

"No, he just left."

"Oh, can you have him call me? Or I'll try his cell. I need to talk to him about something."

"Dad?"

"Yeah, oh . . . so you know all about that?"

"Duh." How does he not know that I know? He left the country, not the galaxy.

"Mom said they talked to you, but she never told me everything they said. So how do you . . . how do you feel about it?"

"How do you think I feel?"

"Righto. How's he doing?"

"He had to go to a Specialist."

"Righto again."

"What's with the righto?" I ask.

"I think I picked it up from my roommates."

"So accents are contagious."

"Highly." He pauses. "How about everyone else? You know, this may not be my place to say this because I'm not the one who is sick or even there but . . . I told them to tell you about Dad. Back when they first told Trent and me. I knew you could hack it. I knew you could help them."

I switch the receiver to my other ear, then switch it back. Honestly, I was like nine when he graduated high school. He always seemed so much older and so smart and I was just a kid. But he's treating me like an adult.

Caleb's sigh stretches across the Atlantic. "Trent moving home and Mom quitting work . . . I don't know if it's really helping. That might be awful of me to say, but I thought about moving back and decided it wasn't right. It's supportive, don't get me wrong, but I realized Dad isn't on his deathbed. He can live with MS. I think he'd prefer that anyway, not feeling responsible for changing everyone else's life. The thing now is, we—the family—all need to live with it. Does that make sense?"

"Yeah. It does." The phone beeps. "Hey, I've got another call, can you hold on?"

"I'll let you go. Just tell them to call me. And hey, if you ever need to call too . . . I know we don't usually talk but . . . it's nice hearing a Yank accent every once in a while."

"Sure. Cool. Thanks."

He clicks off and the other line beeps again.

I don't even have time to think about what just happened, how there's a sibling living on another continent who I hardly know who gets me better than anyone in this house. Having that conversation with Caleb, which might actually have been our first one as quasi-adults, gives me a little push to click over.

"Hello?"

"Sunshine?" Dad. Well, we're just getting right to the point here, aren't we? No Mom to buffer the news. Almost three months spent not going THERE, to the unknown of MS and now we're about to go THERE. And I only hope we can still go back.

I swallow. "How's San Fran?" I ask, artificially bright.

"Well," he begins slowly. "We haven't seen much of it. We went straight from the airport to the hotel to the doctor."

Sirens wail in my brain. It's coming. I can't stop it. "Oh, well, is the weather nice?" I'm peeling the Band-Aid off hair by hair.

"Rainy."

"Oh. I'm sorry."

My dad laughs. "What for?"

"The rain. You hate rain."

"It didn't bother me because I was inside. With the doctor. The Specialist."

Dun dun dun. The Specialist. I hold my breath. Years pass. Babies are born and grow into men. Empires rise and fall. And finally, after seventy eternities end, I exhale. "What did he say?" says a tiny voice I know is mine, although I'm so disconnected from my body I don't feel like I actually asked it.

239

"Well, there's good news and bad news. Which do you want to hear first?"

"I don't want any news," I answer automatically. Robotically. I'm a machine that's just had a spontaneous system override. I explode. "Call Trent and tell him."

Then the system crashes and I hang up.

I'm breathing like I just finished the first quarter of a game. I was ready, I was moving ahead but then talking to Caleb plus the idea of bad news has sent me reeling back to January. How does this Specialist dish out bad news all day when I can't even face it once?

I can't.

Sobs burst out of me. I reach my hand into my pocket and come out with Mr. Nippers's drool toy. I sniff it, an act that only confirms my deeply rooted disgust of cats. What a stupid toy. What a stupid idea. A Focus Object.

The phone rings again and again and again. We don't have an answering machine, so the ringing never stops. I throw the mouse at it, knocking the receiver out of the cradle. This rodent has some sort of magical power, forcing me to answer against my will. Dad's asking if I'm there, and I finally pick up the phone and say I am.

"Payton?"

"What?"

"Don't hang up," he says softly. "Listen. I need you to listen. I have to make this right. Can you at least give me the chance to do that?"

I pluck up the cat toy again and stroke it. It's kind of cute, for a disease carrier. The one eyeball could almost pass for endearing if it wasn't so creepy. "Okay."

"Sometimes parents do things, pretending they're protecting their children, but they're really just protecting themselves. It's not that I didn't trust you. It's more . . . if I told you, it made it real. Irreversible. So I kept putting it off. That was a huge mistake. But it is real, honey. I can't change that. I can't change this. I'm sorry."

He pauses but I don't answer. I dangle the mouse by its tail, watching it spin in a circle. Spinning and spinning until it hit me. Not the mouse. This: I wasn't mad at my dad for lying. Not really. That wasn't why I wasn't talking to them and avoiding spring break plans and wearing his T-shirt and being generally horrible. I spun the mouse again. It was fear.

Because a circle is endless. It goes on forever.

My dad, however, will not.

"So are you ready to hear the news?" he asks.

It takes me a few attempts to answer. My voice has mysteriously disappeared. "I don't think I can."

He chuckles dryly. "It's really not that bad."

"All right. I understand but . . . can we take a break? For tonight? Maybe when you get home, after I've done the bike ride. That's the right time. But right now, can we just not talk about it?"

"Talk about what?"

"Talk about . . . oh, you were . . ." Wow, can he be any more wonderful? "Yeah. Nothing."

"I would love to talk about nothing with you all night long. Just as long as we are finally talking."

So we do. Well, it's not nothing—I tell him ridiculously specific details about the bike ride, and it's not all night long, just twenty-five minutes until Dad hangs up to call Caleb. But those are twenty-five more minutes than we've talked in weeks, in months, and they are twenty-five minutes that communicate much more than the height of my handlebars. When we're done, I go upstairs to lie down and wait for Trent. Dad's T-shirt is still tucked under my pillow.

Jac's right. He's here. No matter what the news might be, my dad is still here.

I wad the shirt up into a ball, fake left, then slam-dunk it into the hamper.

TWENTY-NINE

The first thing I see when I walk into the volunteers and bikers Sub Bash is a sub sandwich piled high with every processed meat imaginable, spanning across an endless buffet table. I'm a big fan of deli meats, the farther from an actual animal the better, so I take this as a good sign. The next thing I see is Grady next to it, a piece of bologna dangling from his chin. This is not a good sign. This is a very bad sign. As far as signs go, this is the worst, like every demonic sign rolled into one.

Jac's next to me in a second, tapping me on my shoulder like a famished woodpecker. "Did you see how much prime meat there is here? And I don't mean the sub. The paramedic table alone is enough to fill a shirtless calendar spread. I met this guy, Ryder—how cool is that? His name is RYDER—and he said I can help out at the booth. Me. Like Florence Nightingale over here."

"Jac. Look." I nudge my head toward Grady.

Jac snarls. "Tell me that isn't Grady the Goth inhaling a slice of salami at a charity event."

"I think it's bologna."

"I think it's disgusting. Why would Grady be here, unless . . ."

Her voice trails off as we see Sean punch Grady on the arm and shove a pickle into his mouth. It makes all the sense in the world and none at all. Of course Sean's doing the bike ride. I'll see him tomorrow. I can see him right now. Did he know I'd be here? Did he care either way?

"Maybe we should go." I turn to leave.

Jac starts poking me again. "I've figured you out, you know. I've been reading all my mom's self-help books. I should write one someday. And if I do, I'm going to write a whole chapter on this self-sabotage stunt you're pulling."

"Thanks."

"Seriously. He's right there. And you're like, denying yourself of him. Torturing yourself. The only way to get out of it is to go talk to him."

"You're right."

"I am? I mean . . . of course I am." Jac pretends to swoon. "Eternal love! You're going to talk to Sean!"

"No. Grady."

"Uh, Grady. As in the not-cute one with a skull on his sweatshirt?"

"Uh-huh."

"I meant Sean."

"I know you did. But I have to talk to Grady first."

Jack sighs. "Maybe I'll write two chapters on you then. Self-sabotage and going after the wrong guy. All right. Do you want me to come along?"

"Yes. But you can't."

"I'll pretend to understand. But, either way, you'll need this." Jac crosses me like she's a priest.

"What's that for? You're not Catholic. Isn't that like, blasphemous?"

She jerks her head toward Grady. "Saving your soul, potato. Can never be too cautious with that boy."

I cross the room and stop at the end of the mile-long sandwich. I busy myself with the condiments, spreading the hoagie with a mayonnaise-mustard combo. I watch them from the corner of my eye, waiting to be noticed so Sean can make up his mind whether he'll stay or leave when he sees me.

My sandwich is inches away from my mouth when I feel Sean's penetrating gaze. Before, I would have dropped the sandwich and fled. But now, I take a small bite, chewing deliberately, and finally make eye contact.

I don't know why I ever thought his head was big. It's perfect, and so is he in every way possible. He's wearing a fitted forest green shirt, one that shows off both his biceps and eyes in equally tantalizing ways. His hair looks white in the lighting—white and brilliant. The only thing that would make him better looking would be a smile, which is completely absent from his face. But he's not frowning. His lips are a straight line, not committing either way. We're staring at each other, and I lose the contest when I look down at my food. When I look up again, he's gone.

But Grady isn't. And although I want so desperately to run after Sean, I have some beef to settle with Grady first.

When he sees me, his eyes dart around the room, trying to find Sean. Or maybe a coffin he can hide in.

"Hey, Grady. Great sub, huh?" I take a mammoth mouthful.

Grady looks down at his sandwich, then up at mine. He follows my motion, shoving as much meat in his mouth as he can, then mumbles a "Mmph."

"I didn't know you were a philanthropist. What brings you to this lovely event?"

He continues to chew, focusing on his black Vans. Finally he swallows and says, "Sean wanted me to come with him. Free food, you know."

"I hope you choke on your bologna," I say.

Grady takes another bite, his expression more thoughtful this time. "Actually, I think it's salami."

"Why did you tell Sean about my journal?"

Grady chokes on his deli meat and coughs. I grab a water bottle from the cooler below and consider splashing him with it, but my curiosity drives me to hand it to him instead. He gulps it down in three seconds, and smears his face against his dingy gray sweatshirt. "So *that's* why Sean and you aren't talking?"

"No." That was my own doing. "But you didn't help things."

Grady's face is about the same color as his sweatshirt now, and he looks like he's close to tears, which would not only smear his liner, but go against everything I thought I knew about him.

"This is so jacked. I had no idea I screwed things up for you guys. *That's* why Sean's been so depressed. I can't believe I did that to him. I'm such a freaking screwup!"

"I don't know if I'd say freaking—"

"Typical. This is so typical." He looks up at the ceiling. "Two hours ago my dad chucked a beer bottle at me because I forgot to take the trash out, now I'm mooching free food from people in wheelchairs and ruining Sean's sad love life."

And then he does it. He starts to cry. Not sobs or anything, just a trembling chin and a few silent tears. And it is SO not the reaction or the interaction I was expecting, that all I can do is awkwardly pat his back and say, "You're not a screwup."

He mumbles a few choice words before raising his head, his eyes wild. "What do you know? I'm *completely* screwed up. My parents destined me to be a screwup—look at any family study, and there I am. The statistic."

"Grady, that doesn't mean—"

But I can't stop him. He's really going now. "Yeah, a cliché. If this were a teen movie, I'd be the stock character." He wipes his eyes and moans, "Dude, my makeup is even running. Can we get any more unoriginal? Next thing I'll be trying out for the part of teen shooter in some TV show."

"Oh, no, they wouldn't cast you in that. All the teens on those shows are really twenty-five. And they just take models and try to nerd them up, you know? Not that you aren't good-looking enough, I just mean even that isn't really authentic. Those actors are more pretty boy James Dean than Marilyn Manson. Not that you're Marilyn Manson. Unless, uh . . . you want to be."

"Yeah, that helps. You really suck at this, you know that?" Grady mops his face with a used napkin, transferring mustard to his left eyebrow. It makes him so vulnerable that for a second I let all his black armor melt away and I see him as just a regular guy, a guy who's a little whacked out but hello—join the club.

I analyze my sandwich. "You know none of that is true. Look, I am . . . I was mad at you but, actually, Sean thought it was all kind of funny. What happened, the reason we aren't talking . . . it wasn't you who messed things up. It was all me."

"How was it you?"

"I did the whole run-away-Lassie thing."

"You impersonated a dog?"

I shake my head. "I knew we were just setting ourselves up for the inevitable, so I broke things off now. Before things got too intense."

"Then you're an idiot if you think that." He rubs his eyes again. "I can't believe I cried. You must be channeling excessive estrogen with all that relationship crap. Too intense. That's the stupidest thing I've ever heard."

And just like that, I distinctly remember why I left the Hall of Terror after our first cheery encounter. "Shut up," I say. "Don't make me change my mind about you."

"And don't make me change my mind about you. Not liking someone because you might get burned later? Haven't you heard the quote ''Tis better to have loved and lost than never to have loved at all'?"

I snort. Another shattered notion. Now Vampire Boy is getting literary. "Uh, all right, Shakespeare."

"Try Lord Tennyson. Just because I'm not on the honor roll doesn't mean I'm not smart enough to know that you should talk to him. You think hurting him like this is doing any good?"

I shrug.

He pushes up the sleeves of his gray hoodie, revealing a Sharpie tattoo that resembles an eagle's claw. He closes the gap between us in one broad step. I can smell the Dijon mustard on his breath. "Fine. We'll do this the hard way. If you don't make things better with my friend, I'll bite you again."

I stiffen. "Seriously?"

"You want to find out?"

I sigh. "So I get to tell him how I feel and have him tell me I already missed my chance. Goody."

"You just said goody."

"So?"

Grady grabs two more sandwiches and starts to scoot away. "I better go. All that wholesomeness might rub off on me."

"Yeah, next thing you know you'll be attending a charity event, quoting poets, and bawling your eyes out."

"That kid is my best friend. You better make things right again or . . ." Grady gives me one more hearty fang flash and disappears into the crowd. And now he's weaved into our collective fate, which may sound poetic and all but . . . it's Grady. I just received love advice from Grady the Goth.

I take another bite of bologna. Or maybe it's salami. Doesn't matter. Suddenly everything tastes like cardboard.

PFE
April 5
Topic: A prayer

I don't think God reads my PFEs but since I'm not really accustomed to praying, I thought I'd

249

get it down here. Ahem. I mean . . . Dear God. Hey. Just a few things. Grady's probably talking to Sean and please let him say something helpful. Please give me the courage to face Sean. And this impossible bike ride. And my dad's disease. And my dad. Please help me move away from all this Focus Object stuff so I don't develop a feline fetish or some other bizarre coping mechanism.

Instead, just help me to cope.

Please?

THIRTY

The alarm rings at four. As in four AM. The four that happens in the morning. The four that no sane person ever sees because they're nestled in bed, not squeezing into spandex and polyester. Not coughing down an organic protein bar. Not spewing it up five minutes later.

I have no idea what sort of warm-up I'm supposed to do for this race. I do my basketball stretches on the cold kitchen floor in the vain hope it'll wake me. Trent wakes up all by himself. Well, partially. He downs two cups of coffee before he even acknowledges my presence, and then all I get is a nod toward the garage.

I'm a pretzel of nerves. The car ride to the city is spent second-, third-, and fourth-guessing my decision to do this race. It doesn't really prove anything. Spinning the bike pedals isn't going to perform any voodoo magic that will heal my dad. All that spinning the bike pedals is going to do is make me incredibly sore, which is actually counterproductive to the whole healing ideal.

The Camden fairgrounds are a mass of wheels, neon, and perfectly sculpted calves. Every one of the hundreds of cars has a bike rack, some with people stretching nearby, or tying up their shoes or clipping on helmets. Teams of riders, some hundreds strong, converge in their designated tents, their matching jerseys demanding intimidation. There's a tent for the police department's team—not the donut-inhaling variety, the kind that make you actually want a traffic ticket. There are business companies, consulting firms, pharmaceutical salesmen. The pink jerseys with bright daisies on the sleeves are the uniform for a local flower shop. The asphalt and buzz of the crowd warms us all some, but not enough to stop the bite of an early April morning.

"Sure you don't want me to stay?" Trent asks as he drags my bike out of the backseat.

"There's nothing for you to do. Just keep your cell on and I'll call when I decide I'm done."

"So when you make it to Ocean City."

"IF I make it to Ocean City. Let's not set unrealistic expectations. I'll do what I can. I've never gone seventy-five miles before."

"You will." Trent yawns and stretches. His shirt creeps up and reveals his swimmer stomach. A girl in the car over gawks. That's my brother, I say. With my eyes. "So am I supposed to give you a pep talk or anything?"

"What you just said is fine."

"Cool."

"Cool." I kick the bike tires, checking the air for the millionth time.

Trent hops from one foot to the other. "Do we need to hug now?"

"No. Would you leave?"

"Good." Trent smiles. "Because I have a lunch date with Yes. And that chick next to us is checking me out and I don't want to ruin her dreams by hugging my little sister."

"Her dreams are preserved. Go home." I click my shoes into my bike, standing on the pedals as I leave Trent to his admirer. Since I am a team of one, Payton Power we'll call it, or the Gritas Grenadier, or just plain old Payton Gritas—wannabe biker and freaking scared girl, I don't latch on to any of the groups but instead weave through the crowds to the sign-in table. I click out of my pedals and stash my bike in one of the many racks so I can get into line.

I spot the G–H line one second, and Sean standing at the end of it the next. The alphabetical connection never ends. From school lunch lines to major bike rides. He can't escape me. I can't escape him.

At first I think he just doesn't see me when I offer a small wave. But after standing two people behind him for over seven minutes, I know I'm being ignored. I count the many bruises on my legs, looking for meaning in their shapeless shapes. It's all so stupid, acting like we aren't ten feet away from each other. Acting like we weren't kind of, sort of, but not really, a couple.

Sean signs in and attaches his number to a jersey so brightly orange, he could hop off his bike and direct traffic. The lady at the table hands him his red bandanna, the bandanna that symbolizes you're riding for someone with MS. Most people here are doing the ride for fun. There's only a sprinkling of bandannas in the crowds. Sean loops his through a hole in his helmet and ties it into a Boy Scout–worthy knot. Even though the orange shirt is the attention-getter, the bandanna is what sticks out. Maybe it's the way he's tied it. Maybe it's just because it's on his head.

He turns around and because I'm staring at him, he can't help but make eye contact. His face is blank, like there is a force field separating us. A force field I created.

This is stupid. We can talk! Just because we aren't . . . whatever we were . . . doesn't mean we can't be civil.

"Good luck," I say. Not that he needs luck. He's Hercules.

He nods, the bandanna nodding as well. "You too."

"Thanks."

"Uh-huh."

It's my turn in line and the lady is tapping her pen, waiting for me to move up. I shift to the side of the line so the next person can go, a bold move indicating I still want to talk to Sean.

"You doing the whole thing?" I ask.

"I'm doing the hundred. With the added loop. Not riding it back though. I've got to be back tonight."

"Oh really? Why?"

"I have plans."

Plans. *Plans* is the polite word you use when you don't want to say what you're doing or don't want to invite the other person along. Like to a party. Or a date.

"Oh."

"How long are you riding?" Sean is no longer looking at me, but past me, like he wants the conversation to be done. He takes some sunglasses out—the funky kind that curve around his face, the style all the pro cyclists wear—and slides them on.

I didn't know the answer before he asked it. But when he looks away like that, like I've accomplished my bizarre goal, like he's really moved on, I answer. "Here to the shore. One way. The seventy-five miles."

He startles. "Really? Are you sure?" I might be deliriously hopeful, or hopeless, but I think I detect worry in his voice. "This isn't a ride around Valley Forge. Serious athletes who have trained for months aren't able to finish."

"I've done Valley Forge, hill and all, hundreds of times now."

A smile flicks across his face. "Hundreds?"

"Well, I haven't exactly counted. Maybe forty-five. I started tripling up in the end. No, I went last weekend, so forty-eight? And I did three rides to the city and back, although last weekend I took a shortcut—"

"Why are we talking?" Sean asks.

I blink. "Why? What do you mean?"

"I mean, I distinctly remember you saying you didn't want this. And Grady told me you compared me to a dog last night. And now you're going on like nothing's happened."

"I didn't compare you to a dog! Tell him he's a lousy middle man."

Sean lets out a loaded sigh and scratches the back of his neck. I want to shrivel up. He so doesn't want to talk to me. "What's the story, Payton?"

The story is I still like you but I'm not sure what's best for us. I'm not sure if I'm best for you, or if I should ever let another person into my life. I'm not sure I even deserve you, just like I

255

really don't deserve my dad. The only thing I deserve is your annoyance, which is killing me. "I don't know. I wish I did."

Sean's face goes soft for a moment. "I wish you did too." Then he shakes his head, like he's shaking away the thought. "Look, I hope you have a great ride. If you want to talk, really *talk* afterward"—he pauses and tugs at his helmet straps—"I'll be around." He pedals away.

He'll be around. He's still around.

I zip right back in line, ignoring the accusatory stares. I have to get my sign-in time ASAP. I have to be as close to Sean as I can. Keep him in sight. Use his head to clear my own. Figure out what I want to say, if there even *is* anything to say. The only thing separating me from talking to him is a few hours. A few hours and seventy-five fun-filled miles.

THIRTY-ONE

There is no gunshot to start the race. What a relief. I've always worried where the bullet goes that gets shot. We have helmets on, so we should be safe there, but there are all those limbs, and the possibilities of a ricochet or misfire and thus multiple casualties.

So no gunshot. It's pretty anticlimatic, actually. Just a lady standing at the start line, organizing each group into their start times, which are five minutes apart. Mine isn't scheduled until later, but I sneak into the one after Sean's, which is a slew of geneticists with double helixes gracing their shirts. Everyone just starts riding, so I don't know if there was a *Hurrah! Go get 'em!* Or just a "Go." I ditch the science geeks, intent on finding Sean. This is no easy feat with the endless stream of bikers around us, not to mention I have to pass them all to catch up.

The ride follows a four-way, sometimes two-way road that winds from Camden, which is just across the Delaware from Philadelphia, through the forest and scattered cities of New Jersey, over two massive concrete bridges, and into Ocean City.

The road we begin on is larger, and cars cautiously cruise by us as the bikers converge from a solid mass into more uniform lines. Those drafting lines lessen the air resistance, making it easier to pedal. I haven't had that advantage in my solo riding, not to mention the terrain is mostly flat.

I thought I was in shape when I played basketball, but I can feel a new strength in my muscles, in my calves. The promise of endurance and ability and greatness. I am a cyclist now. There's no escaping the fact that this is a sport and I am an athlete.

I zip past rider after rider, looping in and around the bulk of wheels until I see Sean's head, and the helmet with the bandanna flapping along. I'm so mesmerized by Sean, I almost rear-end the biker in front of me.

It's weird I still react like this. It's weirder that I went so long NOT reacting like this, that I saw Sean day in and day out for years without once thinking about what I was seeing, or who was beyond what I was seeing.

Sean skips the first rest stop. *Ugh. Slow down! You're not doing the Ironman yet.* But I still follow, staring longingly at the Gatorade the volunteers distribute.

I settle into my groove and alternate between gazing at Sean's bandanna and surveying the surroundings. Spring is on the cusp of springing, and although the trees are still mostly bare, a few buds pop out against the bleak landscape. I notice a biker next to me wearing a Marines jersey. He's a real bulldog, forty-something, so chiseled he makes Sean look like a puppy.

Sean slows down ahead of us. I love puppies.

Bulldog's bike is deluxe, with a smooth, lightweight design

I vaguely remember. I've seen the bike before. At the bike shop Sean and I went to the day we ditched class.

I can remember everything Sean had described about the bike. How the handlebars were more compact and the seat more narrow. How I could carry it with my pinkie it was so light. I listened so intently at the time, desperate to keep my mind busy and away from thoughts of Miss Marietta and her dad, of whom I knew no details. Like, what was his name? What did he do for a living? What was his relationship like with Miss Marietta? These are the normal things you think about when someone dies. You don't focus on alloy wheels. Just like when your dad gets sick you don't spend your energy on a cute boy's head.

But I'm making up for it. If I really do the seventy-five miles, I can earn enough money to make the Silver Donations list. I can go to my dad and say, look how much I raised. I'm with it. I'm here. I'm here for you. And we can talk about what we should talk about. I can do it. I can. Soon.

We come to the second rest stop. I wobble off my bike, ready for a break. Sean wheels over to the sport drinks, grabs two, and downs them both in the amount of time it takes me to remove the cap. He's not looking at me, but I'm all right with this. I'll get his attention when I cross the finish line.

I'd hoped to take a good twenty-minute break, but Sean's back on the bike after ten, and when your Focus Object goes, you follow. Even with the short rest, I feel revived. Giddy. I'm more than halfway there. I have a head to use as a compass. I've got this thing. It's mine.

Then, five miles from the rest stop, I see a sign that says,

LOOP AND FIFTY-MILE MARK: FIVE MILES. The loop. Sean's doing the loop—the extra course that adds twenty-five miles to the ride. I'd totally forgotten about it. Now Sean will be gone and I'll have twenty-five miles of nothing to look at but the Garden State.

I can see the turnoff ahead. For every biker that turns, there are five that go straight. I won't be alone when Sean turns. I can just stare at someone else. Or just think about something else.

Except I can't. Sean makes the turn and I'm instantly paralyzed, watching his bandanna as it disappears around a corner. All I see now is failure. As a safety precaution, I pull off to the side of the road to get my bearings and figure out what to do.

I don't do *anything* for a good fifteen minutes. Taking the break helps my nerves, but with each second that ticks by, it's harder and harder to get going again. I could end now. I did fifty miles, that's something to be proud of. Trent can come pick me up and—

No. The first time I did Valley Forge, I never thought I could FINISH it. Especially not alone. Besides, it's a much hillier ride than this. Shorter, of course, but I also never had drafters. I can think of this as an elongated Valley Forge. I didn't have a stupid bandanna to look at back then. And I did it.

I'll count to ten. When I hit ten, I'll start biking again. When I hit ten, I'll be on the road, headed toward that oasis instead of looking back at the panther. Or jaguar. I can't remember. Whatever jungle beast is going to get me going again.

Ten comes and goes. So does a hundred. Yet I'm still in the ditch, counting my little heart out. I totally want to do this. I do. But for some reason, my body doesn't.

I take off my helmet to tug my ponytail tighter and touch my bandanna. The bandanna I'm wearing because I know someone with MS.

I rub it between my fingers. It's soaked with my sweat, but still has some brand-new crispness. This is the bandanna I should be focusing on. Not Sean's.

I keep massaging the bandanna, images of the past few months flashing in my head. Mom holding that needle, Dad trying to shoot hoops, the picture of Sean on his mom's website. My Focus Journal.

More time passes. I'm not sure how much.

My Focus Object is gone now. If I want to get through this I need to just . . . focus. Period. Finish this thing.

I can do it.

Me, all alone.

I slide the bandanna off and shove my helmet back on. I tie the material through the front slit, so the tips cover my forehead. It's like dangling a carrot in front of a pony so it will move. And I do. I move.

Actually, I fly.

I spend the next twenty-five miles soaring. The bandanna absorbs my sweat as I pass biker after biker. It absorbs my tears as I cross the first bridge that leads us into Ocean City. Not that I'm looking at it now. There's way too much going on.

Purple and green balloons arch gracefully over the people-lined main street. Everyone slows here, taking in the applause and cheers. There are signs saying, THANK YOU FOR BELIEVING! or THIS ONE'S FOR CHARLIE or BIKE YOUR BALLS OFF with a picture of a guy biking in a Speedo. And even the weird Speedo poster inspires me. I don't know a single soul in the crowd. I don't need to.

The bikers ahead of me thin out and I can see the finish line. I stand up on my pedals and cruise across, pumping one arm (not two; "look mom, no hands" is a recipe for disaster) up in victory. The moment's so sweet, there should be music playing. Stand up and dance music like in classic teen movies, where the crowd would rush out and carry me away. But first, my dad would show up and tell me he's cured and Sean would interrupt our father/daughter hug to give me a kiss. Then, the carrying away part would continue until I do one final arm thrust in the air and the credits roll.

But it's not a movie. Three other people cross the same time as me. A smiling, bouncy girl hands me a plastic medal. And now it's done. I slow down and stop, taking note of what everyone else is doing. They're off their bikes stretching and chatting as if they'd simply strolled down the beach, parking their bikes on a nearby rack. I set my bike down on the grass and make a beeline to the Porta-Pottis. Now that the adrenaline is wearing off, I realize how bad I have to pee.

When I'm done, I walk down to the beach. It's still too cold to swim, but there are a scattering of people. I take off my shoes and walk barefoot along the shore, settling down into a partially secluded spot to call Trent.

"Hey," I say when he answers. "I'm done."

"Where are you?"

"Sitting on the beach, right by the finish line."

"Hold on a second. I have a beep." He clicks over for a few seconds, then whistles when he's back on. "So you finished it."

"Was there ever a doubt?"

"Not from me. You ready to go home?"

"Yeah, can you come get me?" I ask.

"Nope."

"Why not?"

"I arranged alternative transportation."

"Trent, this isn't funny. I've biked seventy-five freaking miles. My butt's hurting, my legs are dead, and I just want to sleep for a few days. Will you please come? Now?"

"No can do, little sis. Be glad. Your ride is already there."

"Where?"

"Look around. You'll see him."

"Him? Trent, who is it?"

"What? What? I can't hear you. The phone's cutting out . . . You must have bad reception. What's that? What's that—" He hangs up.

He better not have sent a slacker friend. Just what I need, a few hours of loser BO and whiny punk rock after—

"Hey, sunshine."

I shoot up. My alternative transportation has arrived.

THIRTY-TWO

"Dad? What are you doing here?"

Dad still has his cane, but he's not leaning on it too much. His face seems to have a lot more color than before he left, but maybe that's just me being hopeful. "Your mom and I caught the red-eye. We wanted to see you."

"Oh." I blink, still shocked to see him. "Thanks. Here I am."

Dad looks me up and down, taking in my messy hair and sweaty clothes. "So, can you believe you just biked across Jersey?"

"No. Yes. It's crazy, huh?"

"That's some major money for the charity, right?"

"Enough that Trent's going to regret his two dollar a mile pledge."

"What's the bandanna for?"

"This?" I untie it from my helmet and hold the bandanna up in the sunlight. "They give us these to show we're riding for someone."

"Can I see it?"

"Sure. Sorry it's sweaty."

Dad sits down, placing his cane next to him in the sand. I follow. He wraps the bandanna around his wrist. "I had a coach who used to say, 'There's nothing sweeter than sweat.'"

He loops his arm over my shoulder and we watch the waves in silence. We've had so many silences between us these last few months, bitter ones, loaded ones, empty ones, and hurtful ones. This one is perfect. It says things that words can't.

"You ready to go?" He brushes sand off his slacks.

"Wait, is that it?"

"Isn't it?" Dad looks around. "Do they give you a trophy or something?"

"No, I mean, aren't we supposed to talk about last night and stuff?"

"I don't think there are any supposed to's."

"But you know, dad and daughter on beach." I motion toward the waves. "Triumphant moment. Tears. Hugs. Fuzzy fade-out."

"That sounds like a lot of drama."

"I might have gotten it from a made-for-TV movie."

Dad laughs. "All right. You sure you want to hear it?"

"Yeah." I tuck my head onto his shoulder and swallow. "Go ahead. I think I'm ready now."

"So. The most encouraging part is that my symptoms are lessening. They're switching my meds, hoping it'll decrease the frequency and length of my relapses. The trials they've done on this new med show promise. We'll see what happens when I go back in a few months."

"That's it?" I ask.

"I don't know if that'll ever be 'it.' At this moment it is. Tomorrow can be a different story."

"I hate that part."

"So do I, kiddo." Dad grabs some sand and lets it slip slowly from his hand. "Another thing. Your mom and I got talking, and she's decided to go back to work. Maybe she can be a docent at an elementary school or something. Trent'll get back on his scholarship and start school in fall. We're going to try living our regular lives again, only slightly modified. We'll see how it goes."

"Where do I fit in with that?"

"That's why I'm telling you this up front. You decide. No more choices made without your involvement. Does it sound like something you can do?"

I don't say anything at first. Dad picks up another fistful of sand and it waterfalls out of his hands, grain after grain.

"Okay. Here it is. My contribution is going to be getting over myself," I say. "I mean, I can do normal. Adult normal, though, no more silent treatment or freaking out. I let you know what's going on with me—"

"And I'll do the same," Dad finishes. "Look, everything I said last night still applies. It was awful that we didn't tell you, that we dumped the news on you like we did, and I'm sorry. I made a promise that everything would be okay. It's a promise I might not be able to keep, but I'm going to do my best . . . my best to make things better."

His voice wavers when he says the last line, like he's failed me somehow, and he looks away from me. I grab his hand before he can scoop up any more sand. "Don't apologize. You're perfect, Dad. Seriously, just perfect." I pause to rub my eyes. They are suddenly producing tears. "I know why you didn't tell me. I think I stopped being mad about it a while ago, but I was scared and didn't know how to let it go. I don't know how I'll ever show you how sorry—"

"Hey. How about we make a deal." Dad stands and pulls me up with him. "You let me keep this bandanna and we'll call it good."

"Dad." I wipe at my eyes again. "I didn't talk to you for basically three months and you're going to call it good?"

"Yep."

"So we're good."

Dad smiles. "Aren't we?"

I slide my hand out of his and analyze it. I'm shaking a little from the exertion of the ride. Shaking like my dad's hands sometimes. "I think. Yeah . . . I think we are. I am. I'm good."

"Good."

"Good." I laugh. Then cry. Then laugh some more. "Great."

"Should we go? Bet you're craving some Geno's right about now."

"Actually, I was thinking ice cream." I point to the boardwalk. "There's a place somewhere down there that I heard is decent."

"Ice cream it is then. Or ice cream and Geno's. After that bike ride, you can have anything you want."

We start walking and I pause. "Um . . . first, I kind of need to talk to someone, if that's okay."

"Sean," he says.

"How'd you know—"

"Give me some credit. We may not talk, but I'm not clueless."

"Oh, right."

"I'll head down to the ice-cream shop. Meet me there when you're ready."

My dad breezes away, swinging his cane and whistling a Beach Boys song as he plods through the sand. It's the perfect moment, perfect mental snapshot. I file it in my memory, for moments we'll come to later, for the next relapse or the next Specialist call. Moments not this hopeful, not this warm.

But for now, truly, I'm good.

♥ ♥ ♥

I drift back over to the finish line so I can spot Sean when he crosses. He's a faster rider than me, but he did have twenty-five more miles to cover. So if he averages about twenty an hour, he should be here soon. I take a seat on the sea-misted bleachers and wait.

Ten minutes later: I'm still waiting. The bulldog-looking guy who biked next to Sean crosses. I fix my ponytail and smooth out my shirt.

Fifteen minutes later: I recognize biker after biker, but no Sean. And my dad's waiting. You know, maybe Sean kicked butt and finished before everyone else. I wander over to the food table and survey the crowd. If he's here, I'll see him. I can spot his head anywhere.

Thirty minutes later: I've spanned the length of the food tent twice, checked all the bikes in the racks for Sean's, and still zilch. He's gone. I missed him. He said he'd be around, and he's not.

Sean, and my window of opportunity to make things right, is gone.

♥ ♥ ♥

I ride my bike down the largely deserted boardwalk. Most of the stores are closed until summer, but the ice-cream shop is packed with other bikers. I lean my bike against the outside window and try to push my way into the crowded store.

My dad's sitting at a white wrought-iron table with a mountainous banana split in front of him. He waves and I pull a chair over.

"Sorry it took me so long," I say.

"How'd it go?"

"I couldn't find him. He's probably avoiding me because I screwed everything up. Why do I have to be self-destructo?"

"That sounds like a superhero."

"Not a very successful one. She would blow herself up before she could save the world."

Dad laughs. "Maybe some of her blood will stain her enemies' clothes though."

"Yay. Laundry disasters. My powers are limitless."

Dad shakes his head, smiling. Of course I'm still bummed, but if I can't be better with Sean, at least I can joke around with my dad again. Our spoons clink against the bowl. I'm starving, and the sugar helps a bit. A tiny bit.

"Excuse me."

I turn to the voice, the words jabbing my insides. What's with all these shocking entrances today?

"Sean." I breathe out. He has on a baseball hat and a track-suit over his biking clothes. Dad looks him up and down, a smile playing on his lips.

No one says anything until Sean sticks out his hand. "Hi. I'm Sean Griswold."

"Sorry! Dad . . . this is Sean. Sean Griswold. Meet Sean."

Dad shakes Sean's hand. "Sorry, didn't catch the name? It's Sean, right?"

"Sorry to interrupt." Sean scratches the back of his neck. "I just wanted to let you know . . . I biked for you. I hope that's okay." Sean reaches into his jacket and pulls out his bandanna. "Helps me if I have someone in mind. Here."

"Oh, well . . . thank you. Wow." Dad reaches for the ban-danna. "I'm starting a collection of these. I was actually just about to use the restroom, but why don't you sit down and join us for a bit? There's plenty of ice cream to go around. Payton can tell you all about her superpowers."

Dad gives me a winning smile before he leaves. I shrink into my seat, sweating like I'm back on the bike ride. Gah! Now that I have Sean here, I don't know what to say.

"So, you finished," he says.

"Yeah. Superpowers kicked in around mile fifty."

Someone leans over and asks if they can use a chair from our table and I nod. Sean's phone rings and he looks at the number on the caller ID before turning the ringer off.

"Cool. So I've got to head out," he says, taking a bite of the sundae.

Head out. Sean Griswold's head is out. I have to stop him, say what needs to be said. But I don't say anything.

The table next to us erupts into laughter as a guy tells an animated story to his friends. They all have on the same jersey. There's a fatigued excitement in the air, the kind that appears at the dwindling hours of a slumber party. I almost point it out to Sean. We deserve that. Even if I was stupid before, we could go back to that. Right? Maybe? "Can you stay for a little bit?"

"I can't. I have plans."

"Oh, that's right." I purse my lips together hard so I won't cry.

"My mom has a beach house she's trying to flip down here. My cousins came down for the weekend and we're going to fish and hang out."

"Well, that's great. I hope you have fun. And . . . you should be proud of yourself for . . . you know . . . the bike ride."

"So should you."

"I am." I smile. "I am."

He rubs his temples.

"Headache?" I ask, alarmed.

"No, more like body ache. That second bridge killed me. I haven't had a headache since, well . . . we uh . . . talked about it. I think I just rub my forehead out of habit."

I restrain the urge to burst into song. No more headaches! "You're cured!"

"Cured?" Sean shrugs. "I guess you can say that."

"Well, what did it?" I ask.

Sean points to the sunglasses still on top of his head. "These. My glasses."

"Glasses?"

"Yeah, I was getting headaches from this weird astigmatism. Eyestrain. So the doctor gave me glasses. Well, I just put my contacts in, but these sunglasses are prescription. I wear them riding."

Glasses. Not a brain tumor. Glasses. My freak-out was the result of blurry vision. My own blurry vision.

"They look good on you," I say.

Sean stands. "Thanks. Well, hey, it was good talking to you, but my family's meeting me in the parking lot. Tell your dad I said bye. I'll see you later, I guess."

He nudges through the crowded store. The shop bell rings as he opens the door. I look back at the sundae melting on the table and shovel in bite after bite until my brain freezes. Ah, kryptonite!

Wait, what am I doing? How can I think about ice cream at a time like this? I spring out of my seat and race outside. Sean's halfway down the boardwalk. I run after him and grab his arm. We both stare at my hand, but I don't move it. I think of the last time I stopped him like this, in the hallway when he found out about the PFEs. He forgave me then. Could he do it now?

"I'm wondering if you can help me with something before you leave," I say, out of breath.

Sean nods. I release his arm and draw myself up straight.

"See, I've been thinking about those Revolutionary War soldiers and how they must have been torn, you know fighting the good fight but being away from their families."

"Uh-huh."

"You think they ever got scared, ever . . . ran away? Like, as a self-preservation kind of thing?" I ask. "Even if they knew they weren't supposed to. Even if they really, really didn't want to?"

Sean squints at me. There's so much behind his look—curiosity, amusement, uncertainty. I can feel him though, even from a few inches away, loosening. The edge he's had in his voice is gone. "I bet they did."

"What was the punishment for that? When they got the . . . brains to come back, when they realized how stupid they were. How *sorry* they were. How did they make things better then? Could . . . could they make things better?"

Sean paces the boardwalk, hands behind his back, like a general issuing orders to his troops. "You're speaking of great treachery here. Especially if it's a repeat offense. Trust was vital in the camp."

I hang my head low. I'm an idiot. "I know."

He stops pacing. "But I think the patriots would've forgiven them."

I stop breathing. Could that mean . . . does he forgive me? "Really?"

"After all, those rebels had to stick together, right? How else were they going to win against such huge odds?" He raises my chin. His eyes are endless. His scar is glorious. His hair is sunshine.

His head . . . is heaven.

"So you still think I'm hard-core?" I ask, my voice shaking.

Sean leans in and brushes his lips against mine. There's the taste of peppermint I've been waiting for. I close my eyes and take him in. It's not unicorns or dandelions. It's better. So much better.

"No way," he says, his voice low. "Hard-core doesn't even begin to describe you."

ACKNOWLEDGEMENTS

A robust thank you to:

Sarah Davies, for finding Sean the perfect home and believing in this story despite the absence of tiaras and vampires (oh, wait. So there kind of is a vampire).

Lisa Schroeder, Holly Westland, Angela Cerrito, Shelley Seeley, Rich Wallace, Cynthea Liu, Rachel Hawkins, Sarah Deford Williams, and especially Kristin Daly for reading, critiquing, and guiding me through many drafts.

The publishing dream team at Bloomsbury: Melanie Cecka, Danielle Delaney, Deb Shapiro, Beth Eller, and Alexei Esikoff. Caroline Abbey, Editor of Awesome, for asking just the right questions, understanding/loving the quirkiness, and including enough revision smiley faces to keep me going. It's been an absolute joy to share this bookish experience with you.

My parents for, you know, raising me and stuff. Rylee, Talin, and Logan for being sweet and adorable . . . most of the time. My little sister, Rachel, for reading the manuscript first and loving Sean (even if you insisted I give him dark hair, which was just wrong, wrong, wrong). To my father-in-law, Berne, for answering my questions about multiple sclerosis, and to the National MS Society for helping me understand the complexities of the disease. To Curry, my high school lab partner turned best friend turned husband turned father of my children turned man who helped me write about Valley Forge and bike riding. I never did add a slap-on-the-butt bike crash because no one would be *that* careless. Oh, except, um . . . you. LOVES.